CRYING WOLF

JAMES BUTLER

Little
Island
Books create waves

CRYING WOLF

First published in 2024 by Little Island Books, Dublin, Ireland

A British Library Cataloguing in Publication record for this book is available from the British Library.

Typeset by Rosa Devine
Cover design by Jack Smyth
Printed in the UK by CPI

ISBN: 978-1-915071-50-7

Little Island has received funding to support this book from the Arts Council of Ireland / An Chomhairle Ealaíon

10 9 8 7 6 5 4 3 2 1

*In memory of
my mother Mary Duggan and
my father Jim Butler*

1

Joey is aware of the car before he sees it. He can hear it roll as it pulls into the kerb just alongside him. He glances across his shoulder and notes the make and colour. He knows the car, but wills himself not to know it. He has avoided looking at cars. He has avoided thinking about them. He is trying to forget the list he has in his head like it's some sort of crazy prayer to the maker of cars: Camry, Prius, Chevrolet Silverado, Jeep Patriot, Honda Cr-V, Honda Accord.

But this car has glided to a stop and he can see the full length of it. It's waiting for him. He knows it's waiting. The engine is purring and the indicator light still blinking. He should cross the street and avoid it, but he knows that will only delay the inevitable. There's a bus stop just ahead of him. Maybe the driver of the car – it's a Beamer, gold coloured, the latest in the series – is dropping someone to catch a bus, but you don't use a bus when there's a car like this one available.

Joey passes it by, but hears the slide of the window.

'Hey!' a voice calls out to him. Hasn't he been waiting for this to happen? He turns to look and knows already who he'll see.

It's Quinlan sitting on his own in the back seat. The big brown foreign-holiday head on him like an egg. The eyes are hooded, the two dark arcs of eyebrow the only trace of hair on his face.

'Mr Quinlan!' Joey says like he's surprised. He leans his head to see who's driving.

Weso! What's he doing behind the wheel? And what's with the new look! He's wearing a white shirt open at the neck, with a black waistcoat buttoned up. His black hair has grown, but it's neat now, like he's impersonating a waiter or a professional snooker player.

'So! What's the story?' Quinlan says.

Weso peers straight ahead.

'I'm just going to work. And I'm late,' Joey says. He wants this conversation finished.

'Not much of a job for a lad with your looks,' Quinlan says and Joey doesn't know if he's taking the piss or not. 'What do you get an hour? Minimum wage?'

'Yeah, something like that,' Joey says.

He spots a bus approaching. Quinlan's car is blocking the space but the bus doesn't beep a complaint or attempt to pull in, like the driver knows it's best to keep moving.

'Get in,' Quinlan says, and it sounds like an order more than an invitation.

Joey glances over the car like he's contemplating the distance to his job and the detour he'll now have to take.

He doesn't want to miss work. At the rate he's going he could make employee of the month. Hilarious.

'Will you get in. Wesley will drop you to your job.'

This time he knows it's an order, and he has to obey. You don't fuck with the likes of Quinlan.

'I don't want to be late,' he says across the top of Quinlan's head.

Quinlan sniggers and Weso keeps his statue pose going.

Joey goes around the rear of the car and sits into the back seat, his butt squeaking the soft cream leather. There's a child's book on the floor mat near his feet. He lifts it up. He inspects the cover. It's got the picture of a pink teddy bear on the front.

'Hey, Weso, you left your book back here,' he says.

'Put your belt on,' Quinlan orders, taking the book out of Joey's hand and placing it in the door pocket at his side.

Joey would like to know who the book really belongs to, but you don't ask Quinlan personal questions.

Then Quinlan nods towards the driver's seat and the car pulls out into the road.

Joey doesn't know what to think. The book has thrown him off balance. It's made him remember a different book. That one had a red and yellow cover with the picture of a dog chasing a butterfly. He can't be thinking of that now, not now when he has to keep his wits about him.

He's in the car – with Quinlan beside him – and Weso driving. Quinlan! What the hell does he want him for? Why now? And Weso driving? What's that about? Weso – who never had a good word to say about Quinlan.

But Joey knows deep down what this is about. Of course he does. His stepfather – ex-stepfather really – Vinnie. He looks out the window. This isn't the way to work, he realises. They're heading out of the city, not deeper into it. He is about to lean forward and say something to Weso, but Quinlan places a rough hand on his thigh and squeezes it – squeezes it just a little too hard for comfort.

'Scenic route,' he says.

Joey catches Weso's eye in the rear-view mirror but there's no recognition of him there. He could be anyone now.

He takes his phone from his pocket. He has to send a text to Hazel in the store to tell her he's running late. But how late? That's the question.

2

The car is heading towards his home place. He should text Hazel to let her know it could be ages before he shows up for work. She's going to need to get cover. She's going to do her nut cos she'll have to fill in for him if no one else is available.

'So, how's your ma these days?' Quinlan asks.

'She's fine.'

'Still working in Woodies?'

'Yeah.'

'And your sister?'

'Half-sister.'

'Isabel?'

'Yeah.'

'Another pretty face by all accounts.'

'Yeah, I suppose.'

'And Wesley's sister? Sharon.'

'What about her?'

'I hear she's turned into a bit of a looker. And brains as well!' He glances towards his driver. 'Poor Wesley! He got short-changed in those two departments.'

Joey laughs, then pulls out his phone like he's checking for the time.

'I hear you've left home,' Quinlan says.

'Yeah.'

'In with your Aunt Jackie.'

'Yeah.'

'A row with your auld one, was it?'

'Too big for the nest,' Joey says, trying to keep it light and not show any nervousness. Where are they driving to?

Joey searches the mirror for Weso's eyes, but he's avoiding all eye contact.

The car motors up the bypass and turns right for his estate.

'I don't want to go home,' he says.

The comment is ignored. Quinlan is peering into his phone and smiling at some bit of news he's scrolled into view.

'I don't need to go home,' Joey says to Quinlan, giving him eye contact. He glances away quickly, though.

'Relax, Joey. This won't take long. You'll be back in your job in no time.'

Weso doesn't take the three o'clock off the roundabout for Joey's road, but drives through it and takes the next turn left onto the Green, and then down past his own gaff. Joey can't help but look towards it on the off-chance that he might catch sight of Sharon. But he knows she won't be at home at this time. She's on her way to college. He hasn't heard from her so far today and that's something else he doesn't want to think about.

Weso pulls in at the local shop. The shop is more like one of the houses, but the front room has been converted and it sells the basic foodstuffs, plus it does a good line in cheap cigarettes and sweets and it has a Lotto machine and you can get your phone topped up. Weso lets the engine run and nobody speaks.

As usual there's a group of lads, four in number this time, gathered outside the shop, sitting on a low wall. They're tracksuited and smoking, killing time, probably waiting for some poor sap to come along that they can intimidate. They turn their heads at the sight of Quinlan's car and they move out from the wall to get a better look.

Ginsey is there. Joey recognises him immediately from the crutch, the way he uses it to unfold himself to a standing position. He's waving the crutch round at one of the lads and then he points it towards Quinlan's car. Joey sits back into his seat and lowers his head to check his phone. There's no message from either Hazel or Sharon.

'Put the phone away,' Quinlan orders.

Joey glances at him, then does what he's told.

'Here!' Quinlan says, and when he looks, Joey sees a fifty note in the man's hand. He frowns at it.

'Go in there and get me twenty smokes. You know the ones I want.'

Joey doesn't take the money. 'Get Weso to do it. He's working for you, isn't he?' He searches the mirror once more but it's empty, like maybe Weso is some class of vampire.

'Just get me twenty smokes and buy some for yourself.'

'I don't smoke.'

'You give them up?'

'Yeah. Bad for your health.'

'Sometimes not buying them can be bad for it.'

He holds the fifty between his fingers. Joey stares at it and then takes it. He unclips the seat belt and opens the door. He stands outside the car and stares towards the group of lads. They remind him of hyenas, skulking, waiting for the first sign of weakness. Ginsey is at the front of the pack and he's pointing the crutch in Joey's direction like he's naming his prey. But Joey knows what's going on here. Quinlan is trying to give Joey some sort of message – that's how he operates – and Joey's working it out now, as he walks the path towards the front of the shop.

Ginsey takes up the full path as Joey approaches. He stands in Joey's way and points the crutch at him, this time like it's a sword and he's ready to plant it. Joey has to stop when he reaches the steel tip and it's pressed against his chest. Ginsey's like a rat, with his pointy face and crooked front teeth and the bit of black hair above his lip that seems like he is forever wishing into a moustache. *Mouse-tache*, Joey thinks, but he doesn't smile. There's nothing really to smile about and he puts all his effort into trying not to blink. He does, though, when Ginsey twists the tip so it screws up a piece of his T-shirt. If it was the barrel of a gun then Joey knows he'd be already dead, going by the amount of hate he sees swimming in Daryl McGinn's eyes. He can see the three lads with their shaven heads lost somewhere back in their grey hoodie tops and their dead eyes peering out at him like they're not sure which zombie film they're in. They stand waiting – expecting Ginsey to make a move that will give them today's first buzz.

But Joey knows he doesn't need to speak or be afraid. He turns to show them whose car he's just gotten out of. For a second, he panics, because they can only see the head of Weso. Maybe they think it's a stolen car and he and Weso are still together and it's old times and they're cheeky enough now to be in Ginsey's territory.

Then Quinlan steps out of the back seat and buttons the black jacket of his smart business suit. Joey sniffs at the sight of him. Dress him like the pope and he'd still look every inch a thug.

Quinlan doesn't look at any of them, doesn't even acknowledge anything about where he is. It's like he's out the country somewhere and has gotten out of his car for a smoke. That's what he does. He lights up a cigarette and stares up at the hills behind all the houses. He smokes it with his back turned to them all; like none of them exist, like he would rather be anywhere else than here.

Ginsey lowers the crutch and steps to one side. As Joey moves past him, he can sense the bottled-up hate. He'd like to look him in the eye and tell him he had nothing to do with what happened. It wasn't his idea. It was never his idea and he wasn't even aware that it had gone down until he heard it from Weso.

He walks into the shop and feels relieved there's only one other customer inside, a long-haired young guy, Joey's age, who's also buying smokes. He doesn't recognise him at first because of the hair, but when the lad turns to walk out, he sees it's Magpie Dolan.

'Hey, Magpie, what's da story?' he says.

'Joey!' Magpie barely mouths, with a nod, and then he's out the door and Joey hears the machine-gun cackles and the sneering guffaws that follow Magpie's walk all the way to the road.

Big Richie is behind the counter. His long grey hair is pulled back from his soft doughy face in a tight ponytail. For such a big man he has narrow shoulders. He looks like he's hiding a pillow under one of the extra-large army T-shirts he likes to wear.

'Fucksake, those lads are gonna ruin my business,' he says, shaking his head.

'What business?' Joey says, looking towards the bin of biscuits he knows are well past their sell-by date. Everything in Richie's shop is past its sell-by date – including Richie.

'Don't you fuckin' start.'

'Sorry, Richie. Having a bad day is all.'

'Yeah. I saw the car you came in. Now what can I do you for?'

'Twenty Marlboro Gold, Richie.'

'Where you living now?' Richie asks when he places the smokes on the counter. 'Hey, you still riding that Sharon one? Fair play to yeh.'

'Just the smokes, Richie, OK? I haven't time to chat.'

Richie leans his head to look out the window and grimaces at the hate-filled stares that are shooting towards him.

'Yeah, I can understand that. You want me to call an ambulance or a hearse?'

Joey gives him a brief smile and sniffs.

Richie pushes the smokes towards him and takes the fifty and rubs it with some sort of pen to check it's not fake. Joey turns away from him and surveys the scene outside. Ginsey and his three ghouls are staring off towards the car.

When Joey emerges from the shop, they turn to stare at him, and as he moves past them, they follow Ginsey's slow steps like the pack of dogs they are, just waiting for a command to let them loose. But they stop short of the car. Quinlan turns once he hears the car door open and he flicks the butt of his cigarette to spark off the road. Then he sits into the back seat once more and gives the nod to start the engine.

Quinlan takes his smokes and eyes the change before disappearing everything in his inside jacket pocket. He doesn't say anything. He doesn't need to say anything. The message is clear. Weso is working for Quinlan now. He's protected because he's Quinlan's dog. Joey can be Quinlan's dog too if he gives Quinlan what he wants.

'What do you want?' Joey says.

They have pulled in at the Luas stop. Joey doesn't complain. It's too much to expect that they'd drive him to work. He's just glad to be getting out of the car.

'Your da.'

'He's not my da!'

'Aww! He's slipped down the charts, has he? That's a bummer. And I thought you and him were as thick as thieves.' He laughs then. 'Thick as thieves! Is that funny or wha, Weso?'

'Yeah, that's funny, Mr Quinlan,' the lickarse says.

'I don't know where he is,' Joey says. 'I don't want to know. And neither does Ma or Isabel, so don't be bothering them about him.'

'And Wesley here has no idea either. Seems like the whole world has gone sour on poor Vincenzo.'

'Yeah, well, he knows he's better off staying away from here.'

Quinlan places his phone into his jacket pocket.

'There's a story doing the rounds that your stepda's returned to the big smoke. You hear anything about that?'

'No! And I don't want to hear. And I don't have his number any more in case you think I do. Anyways, what do you want him for?'

'We'll talk again,' Quinlan says and turns away like Joey no longer exists.

Joey stands on the footpath watching Weso turn the car to take Quinlan to his next intimidation appointment. He feels sorry for Weso. How has he let himself become shackled to a thug like Quinlan? But more importantly, how is Joey going to stay clear of him now that he's searching for his stepda? Vinnie. The name has been said, and all those old thoughts come racing into Joey's head. How is he going to be able to forget what happened, if Vinnie comes back into their lives? Ma won't want him anywhere near the house! And if she knew what he had caused to happen she wouldn't want to see Joey back there either. He's not going to be anyone's dog, though. If Quinlan wants to find Vinnie, he can sniff him out himself.

His phone rings. He looks at it, hoping it might be Sharon. But it's Hazel, not happy with his attitude.

3

Joey walks and tries to ignore the parked cars, but he can't shut out the roll call of names.

Camry

Prius

Chevrolet Silverado

Jeep Patriot

Honda Cr-V

Honda Accord

These are the cars Vinnie said that have the best catalytic converters. There are other good choices out there, but these are the premium ones, the ones that make the extra bit of dosh.

Palladium

Rhodium

Platinum

'Are yeh listening to me, Joey? When precious metal prices go up, so does the demand for catalytic converters.

And to possess these precious metals all that's needed is a car surgeon and two assistants all working together as a team. And the operation is completed in sixty seconds.'

To prove his point, Vinnie showed him the YouTube footage of the other experts in the field. Joey wasn't keen to get involved. He'd had his own line of business, selling knocked-off runners door to door, and cheap fags he bought in bulk from one of Quinlan's guys. And at the weekend he and Weso dealt a bit of weed they got off one of Weso's dodgy neighbours.

But Vinnie talked him into it, said he needed someone he could trust, and all Joey'd ever have to do was drive the van and keep watch while Weso jacked the car up and Vinnie slid beneath and carried out the operation.

'The owners don't even know it's gone until they hear the roar the engine makes. But then they just get the exhaust replaced and it's all done through their insurance. And those fucking insurance companies are the biggest robbers of the lot. Do you understand me, Joey? And all those fuckers who have those fancy cars – how do you think they got them in the first place? It's by robbing the rest of us through all the tax dodges they do, and the dodgy deals they make, and the cheap money they can get off those crooked bankers who are screwing us all full time and we just lap it up. So, all we're doing, bud, is getting even.'

Vinnie's voice rattles on in Joey's head like loose change in a tumble dryer. Joey tries to stop the noise by thinking of the pack of hyenas outside the shop and Ginsey's hate-filled eyes. He'd needed two crutches after what Vinnie did to him, but now he's just wielding the one. He's on the mend, so how soon before he goes looking for revenge?

Vinnie's voice intrudes once more.

'He screamed like a baby girl. And he pissed himself. Should have taken a photo of it for the little fucker in case he ever needs reminding to keep his yapper zipped.'

Maybe Joey shouldn't have said anything to his stepda about how he heard Ginsey mouthing off about him – how he knew it was him in the CCTV footage that some nearby householder put up on YouTube. It was the fat arse on him and what a laugh they were all going to have when it appeared on *Crimeline*. Yeah, Ginsey shouldn't have been mouthing off like that, and Joey wasn't the only one who heard him.

Vinnie might have stayed and brazened it out, but he knew that sort of loose talk would have the cops calling to his door. Which is why, he told Joey, he had to rough Ginsey up, stop his mouth.

But why is Quinlan looking for Vinnie now? If he has come back, Joey has to steer clear of him – if they let him steer clear. *Oh fuck, please let me be able to steer clear*, he says in his head.

He doesn't go to work at all. What's the point now when he's heard from Hazel? No smiling emojis there. But Sharon makes up for it with her love-heart eyes and her mouths blowing kisses.

He takes the Luas red line into the city centre then strolls up to Trinity College. He'd asked Sharon should he call her Shasha or some other fancy name now that she's a student in the place. She got in through the Trinity Access Programme, and she's chuffed to be a student. She just loves it. LOVES with capital letters. Great if she felt the same about him. She texted him while he was on the Luas, said that she'd meet him in the Buttery when he was finished his shift in the shop. He's hoping maybe she'll come round with him to his room in Jackie's, but he knows she might not want to do that. She likes Jackie, but feels like she's intruding on her space because her apartment is so small.

There's a clutter of tourists hanging around outside the front gate and Joey pauses to admire the statues they've placed on either side of the entrance. The statue on the right is a man with a book in one hand like he's reading it, and a pen in the other like he's going to scribble something on it. Joey is reminded of the book in Quinlan's car. Then the other book with the dog on the cover lines up beside it in his mind. He doesn't want to think about that book. Did it even get bought for him in the end? But maybe what happened that day was the reason he never got interested in reading. He can't remember the last time he read a book – but he wrote on plenty of them.

He shoulders his way past the tourists and walks through the wooden entrance. He finds himself in another world, like something out of ancient Rome. It's hard to believe there's a place like this hidden in the middle of his city. He stands on the cobblestones and gazes at the beautiful old buildings that surround the square.

Then he realises he's been here before. But it was years ago when he was seven or eight and his ma brought him in to see the Book of Kells. They had to queue for ages and then he didn't know what the fuss was about. A load of old monks with nothing better to do than colouring-in. He had spent a lot of his own time in primary school doing exactly that, but no-one ever made a fuss over his work. Except for his ma, of course, who put the drawings he brought home on the fridge door like he had a talent at least for something.

Ma told him that he could be a Trinity student if he kept his head down and studied hard. Joey never studied hard. He never studied at all, and he didn't stay long in secondary school. He was too busy arguing with teachers and messing when he should have been serious. And Vinnie, when he came along, didn't put any pressure on him to do good in school.

Sharon says he has loads of brains, just never uses them. She keeps telling him he needs to use them now if he wants to be her fella. And she's insisted he come into Trinity to meet her – like it's going to inspire him to do more with his life. But so far, it's having the opposite effect. It's just making him feel stupid.

The buildings are like something out of a Harry Potter film. Students walk past him like they're from that world and he has the invisibility cloak on.

A group of tourists are gathered round a guy with an umbrella and he's talking to them like he's warning them, giving out to them maybe for not being prepared for the weather in Ireland.

Joey starts to think about Quinlan and what he wants. Why the interest in Vinnie all of a sudden?

But he quickly banishes those thoughts and stops a white-haired man with a white beard and glasses, who looks like a professor. He asks him where the Buttery is, but the man tells him he's just taking a shortcut and walks off on him, annoyed like he's been found out. Then two lads in green and gold GAA jerseys come towards him and they don't look like they're Trinity heads, but he asks them for directions all the same, and they point him towards a building in the corner of the square. He checks his phone for the time. He's hours too early, but he'll suss the place out. He's dying for a smoke, but he's told Sharon he'll give them up for her sake. There is so much he wants to do for her sake. He doesn't want to blow it now with any false move.

Quinlan turning up like that has freaked him out. 'We'll talk again,' Quinlan said. It's like the opening move in a game of chess. He reminds himself of his promise not to be dwelling on all the shit that's happened to him in the past. But it was easier to do that when he was taking stuff to numb his brain. Now he can't be that person any more or Sharon won't hang around. He doesn't want to lose Sharon. And he won't – if he keeps his job and stays away from Vinnie and Vinnie stays away from his new life in the city, where he's happily living with his ma's sister.

He's in the door of the Buttery and he's relieved to find it's relatively quiet and looks normal, like a canteen you'd get anywhere. He was expecting long wooden tables and candles and owl shit on the floor.

He buys a coffee and decides at the last second it will be a takeaway one. He carries it outside and sits on the hard cold steps of the building next door that has massive

Roman columns holding up the front of it. Yes, he would love a smoke. Three scruff-bird pigeons venture towards the bottom step like they're expecting a food gift but he has nothing to offer them. The pigeons are probably more entitled to be here than he is, with long squatting rights gained over the years. How long does a pigeon live for? He should know that. If he had stayed on in school, or read more books instead of writing on them, he might have the answer to that.

A man sits down next to him – not too close to cause discomfort. He doesn't know where the man suddenly appeared from. He's in jeans and runners and wearing a trendy navy hoodie that's zipped open and showing off a white T-shirt that has the letters NYC printed on the front. But it's the man's old but well-cared-for runners that catch Joey's attention. They're Gucci Screeners.

'Nice!' Joey whispers to himself. He never sold anything as expensive as Gucci. The man carries a black computer bag and places it on the step beside him, then roots in it. He has black hair cut tight and designer stubble to match. He looks like he's in his late thirties. He could be a student – but what student can afford seven hundred euro runners? He's definitely not a tourist. He takes out a tobacco pouch and rolls a smoke. Joey watches him make all the well-practised movements with his fingers and then there's the final lick and the completed smoke is between his lips and he lights it up and blows smoke away to the side. He offers the pouch to Joey.

'No thanks,' Joey says, not sure if this is what usually happens in a place like Trinity. Are they all friendly fuckers or is he gonna have to give the guy a dig before he walks away?

'Joey! Yeah?' the man says.

Joey turns to frown at him but the man is staring out towards the cobblestones and the buildings on the far side of the square.

What the fuck! he thinks. *Who is this guy?*

Then he knows. There's no badge on show, no blue light flashing, but he knows – he just knows the man is a cop. Joey goes to get up but the man puts a hand out, blocking his lift-off. He could be pointing at something across the way.

'Don't go yet. You need to hear what I have to say.'

Joey doesn't need to hear anything from this guy, but he settles back on the step.

'What do you want?'

'Quinlan,' the man says, peering off into the distance. 'Quinlan!'

'The very man.'

'I don't know anything about Quinlan.'

'But your da does.'

'He's not my da.'

The cop takes a drag from his rollie and blows smoke out in front of him. The breeze blows it back into their faces. Joey draws some of it in as he takes a deep breath. What is it about this day that all this crazy shit is happening? Nothing for about six months and now it's like everyone he meets wants to talk about Vinnie.

Then he turns to look at the cop.

'I don't know anything about my stepda. And I

21

don't want to know. He went off somewhere. Donegal or somewhere wild like that. And he got work in some garage, but nobody knows where exactly, so maybe if you want to find him you should check out the garages up there. And my ma hasn't heard from him either, in case you're wondering. And she doesn't want to hear. He's gone from the house nearly a year ago. Is that enough info for yeh?'

'Thank you, Joey,' the man says. 'That's more info than I expected.' He draws more smoke in from the cigarette, but he's made it too tight so it's going to go out on him. 'And does Quinlan believe you know nothing about your stepda's whereabouts?'

'What the fuck?' Joey says and he jumps to his feet before the man can arm-block him again. He doesn't look back but heads towards the gap between two buildings and he finds himself in another square. There are people sitting at wooden picnic tables in the corner of it, with what looks like a coffee shop behind them. He strides there and heads up the ramp to the right of the tables. Once inside the building he turns so he can watch the gap to see if the cop is following him. There's no sign of him. But that means nothing. There could be someone else taking up the watch. He glances round him but nobody seems to be the least bit interested in him. Outside at the bottom of the ramp there's a young lad in a hoodie leaning over the front of an electric scooter and tapping his phone, but he looks like he doesn't belong in this place any more than Joey does.

'Hey!' he hears. 'Joseph!'

He swivels round and sees Sharon. She's with this guy who has long wavy brown hair and a shadow for a beard. He looks like one of those cool guys from California who live on surfboards. He's got a scarf on, though it's too warm for scarves, and there's a colourful badge on his tweed jacket that has the word 'Pal' on it. How come he notices all this before he can even look at Sharon? She's smiling at him. He wants her to come and hug him, and she must be reading his thoughts because she does. He looks into her eyes and they're smiling at him and registering surprise – but she's comfortable seeing him here even though they're not meant to meet for another two hours.

'I thought you were working?' she says.

'I wasn't needed. Bit of a mix-up with the rota.'

He can see the guy with the Pal badge inching his way forward, wanting to be introduced. Sharon is aware of it also. She takes Joey's hand and pulls him forward.

'Joseph, this is Miles. Miles, Joseph.' They shake hands. Miles's handshake is solid.

'Joseph is my boyfriend,' Sharon says. Her accent is different, suddenly sounding more green line Luas than red.

'But you can call me Joey,' Joey says and gives Sharon the briefest of frowns. What the fuck!

'Lucky guy,' Miles coos and Joey thinks he's gay. He's relieved about that.

'You go ahead, Miles, and I'll follow you up.'

Miles gives her a smile and looks at Joey like he's the luckiest guy on the planet.

'Is he gay?' Joey says, as soon as Miles is out of earshot.

'For fucksake, Joey, you can't say that.'

'What?'

'That can't be the first thing you say about a guy you've just met. There are other, more interesting questions you can ask.' Her accent is back on the red line. 'Jesus, Joey!'

'OK! Sorry!'

She shakes her head at him. 'Miles is giving me a hand with an essay I'm trying to write and then I've a tutorial – so I can't see you for … an hour and a half.'

'That's OK,' Joey says. 'Is that what his Pal sign is about? Is he like one of those guys who greet shoppers in that shoe shop you go to?'

'You're such an eejit, Joey. He's making a statement about Palestine. Miles is interested in all that politics stuff. He's a bit of a genius, actually. He's studying English, and you should hear him speak about Joyce, Heaney and all the other great Irish writers.'

'Whose Joyce Heaney when she's at home?'

'OH MY GOD, JOEY!' She stares at him. 'I know you're messing.'

He gives her a goofy smile, like he knows what she's on about, and she laughs out loud. Heads turn to watch them. He loves the way she laughs. If he could bottle it and carry it round with him then everything would be OK.

'He speaks a bit like yer man!'

'Who?'

'Yer man in that film. The Irish guy.'

'Joey, please! Don't be talking like that in here.'

'What?'

'Yer man! Like – say out who you mean, and leave your man at home.'

'Fucksake, Sharon, I'm just saying he sounds like yer man in that film with the line-up.'

'*The Usual Suspects*, you mean.'

'Yeah, him! That's who yer man – Miles or whatever you called him – sounds like.'

'He doesn't sound like him at all, Joey.'

'OK! Jesus!'

'Listen, I'll see you where we agreed, in the Buttery, if that's OK. But I can't go round to Jackie's with you. I have too much to do tonight. I've another essay to get in by Friday.'

'That's OK,' Joey says, though he's all stirred up now about 'yer man' and calling him 'Joseph' and letting her get away from him early. Then she raises herself up on her toes like a ballerina and she kisses him full on the lips. The suddenness of it makes him go red. Sharon laughs, pushing loose strands of her blond hair behind her ears.

Then she's gone and he touches his lips where she kissed him.

'Fuck,' is all he can say. *How am I gonna hold onto this one?* he thinks, and feels suddenly panicked.

4

Joey has staked out a table in the corner of the Buttery, just inside the door, so he can keep an eye on who's coming and going. Sharon isn't late. She's right on time. He likes that about her. Some girls keep you waiting for ages and you're expected to feel lucky they bothered to turn up at all. But not Sharon. And when she's with you she's with you and not checking her stupid phone all the time like one of the last girls he was with.

She doesn't hug him this time, just sits into the seat beside him and stares about her like she's seeing it for the first time, though she must be in here every day.

'Hey, I still have to pinch myself,' she says, and then her eyes are his again. 'So? What's the story?'

He wants to tell her about the cop outside. He wants to tell her about Quinlan. He wants to know why everyone is interested in Vinnie all of a sudden.

'Do you know Weso is working for Quinlan?'

'Yeah, he told me.' Her face darkens.

He's sorry now he's punctured her bubble. But if he can't float up where she is, she'll have to come down to where he's at.

'I'd prefer if you didn't call him that any more.'

'What? Weso?'

'Yeah. I don't want people in here knowing I have a brother with a name like he's out of the hood or something.'

'All right, but does he know what he's getting into, Sharon?'

'If you sup with the devil, you need a long spoon,' she says.

'What?'

'Have you never heard that before?' she says and smiles, like she has all this secret knowledge. He shows her the small spoon he's used to stir his cappuccino. She laughs.

'Anyway, I'm moving into town, so I don't need to hear what Wesley gets up to any more.'

This is news, but Joey's not sure if it's welcome news yet.

'Where?'

'I'm moving in with Miles.'

She pauses and smiles at the look of shock on his face. 'And his boyfriend.' She laughs out loud as his frown melts and he smiles.

'So, I was right.'

'Yeah. And I've met his partner. He's an artist. Rodney something or other. He's not studying here. He's in art college doing fine art or something like that.'

'Hey, that's great news, Sharon,' he says, wishing he could bring her somewhere where they could be alone together.

'Yeah, it is, isn't it? They need me to help pay the rent, but it's not mad dear so I'm happy out. And they'll be in here shortly so you can say hi to both of them.'

'Just don't give him-from-the-hood the address?' Joey advises her.

'Nobody is getting the address except you,' she says.

He reaches for her hand but stops before he can take hold of her long fingers. His eye catches the Gucci runners and then the navy hoodie as the cop comes in the door and glides past them without looking left or right. Joey dips his head down to the side, but Sharon has noticed his move and she spots the cause of his sudden unease.

'What's going on?'

'Just someone I'm trying to avoid.'

The guy is up at the counter ordering food.

'I've seen him before,' Sharon says, craning her head upwards to try and see him properly.

'Where?'

'Yesterday ... or the day before. The day before! When I was waiting for one of the girls outside the library. He came up to me and we chatted about college life and I told him about the social science course I'm doing.'

'Fucker,' Joey says.

'What? What's going on, Joey?'

'I don't know what's going on. I don't know if anything is going on.'

'Joey, I'm warning you now. If you bring any of your old crap in here, then we're finished. OK?'

'We can't stay here,' Joey says.

'What?'

'Come on, let's get outa here.'

'I'm not going anywhere, Joey. This is my place now. This is my time.'

Then the door opens once more and Miles is there and smiling and coming towards them. Behind him there's a black guy who has to be an artist. If he's not an artist then he's in fancy dress and on his way to a party for artists because he's wearing a black beret and he has a tuft of goatee beard hanging from his chin. He's wearing bell-bottom jeans and a blood-red T-shirt beneath a black waistcoat that has silver buttons down the front.

'This is Rodney,' Miles says to Joey, and Joey stands and shakes the hand that's offered.

'Nice to meet you, Joseph,' Rodney says.

Joseph! There it is again. He'd better knock that on the head before it catches.

'I don't mind if you call me Joey. I'd prefer it in fact.'

He gets a finger poke in the back but ignores it.

'Rodney is from Montenotte,' Miles offers like maybe he's trying to explain something about the lad's accent.

'What part of Africa is that in?' Joey says, as he readies himself to make a getaway. He's worried about the cop. He doesn't know where he has moved to, where he has set up his watch from. All he knows is he can't stay here.

'Oh my God!' Sharon wails and the two lads howl with laughter.

'He's from Cork, you gobshite,' Sharon quickly adds, her face the colour of Rodney's T-shirt.

'I knew that,' Joey says. 'I was only joking.' He stands out of their way, and the two lads think he's being mannerly and making room for them to sit. But he's going now.

'Hey, you're not leaving,' Miles says, like he'll be disappointed if fun boy Joey disappears on them.

'Yeah, sorry but I gotta go to work.'

'Is everything OK?' he hears Miles say to Sharon.

'Just shit about spoons,' she says back, and he knows they don't know whether to laugh or not.

But he's gotta get out into the air where he can breathe again.

5

He's in McDonald's and the place is jammers with tourists. They're making some racket and he's grateful he got his Big Mac and fries on his tray before they swarmed into the place. Now he's sitting in one of the plastic seats with his eye on the door.

He doesn't know what's going on. Quinlan's looking for Vinnie. And now the cops want Quinlan, but they're interested in Vinnie too. Why? What has he got that they want? Or what has he done? Maybe they're only watching the CCTV footage now and want to talk to him about it. Joey has seen it on YouTube. No way anyone could recognise him or Weso. The two of them are hidden in their black hoodies like a pair of Ginsey's ghouls. But Ginsey said he recognised Vinnie's fat arse. Maybe Joey needs to check the footage once more.

He takes out his phone. There's a text from Sharon.

Joey! WTF?

He'd like to think this is about his gaffe over yer man from Cork but he knows her comment is not about that. He texts her immediately.

> Hey! Lookin forward to seein your new gaff.
> Call you later.

Maybe he's blown it with her now, and he may never see the inside of her new place. He knows she's right to be freaked out. That was really stupid what he did, souring her day by making a big deal about the cop.

He leaves McDonald's and heads down towards O'Connell Bridge and then round by the quays and passes Busáras heading for his Aunt Jackie's place. He hopes she hasn't invited her new fella, Martin, around. She said she's keen for him to meet Joey. That means she likes him. He's Jackie's boss and she must have the hots for him bad, otherwise she wouldn't be lighting all those smelly candles. He sniffs at his armpits in case he's the reason for the candles, but all he can smell is his 'Wicked Chill' deodorant that Sharon insisted on buying for him. Two guys zip past him on electric scooters and one looks like the guy he spied in Trinity with his hoodie and black jacket, but then the other guy is dressed the same like all these scooter heads have found a uniform they like to wear.

Jackie should be home from work by now and he needs to talk to her, but he won't be able to do it if that Martin is there.

He opens the metal gate that's just up the road from the train station and finds himself in the little alleyway they use as a shortcut to the small green area where his aunt has her apartment.

'Hey!' he calls out once he's in the hallway.

'In here,' Jackie answers from the kitchen. A strong smell of coffee hits his nostrils.

He takes the few steps down the short corridor and peers into the kitchen. She's at the sink, with her back to him, and she's filling a mug with coffee.

She turns when she hears him.

'We've visitors,' she says and points towards the far end of the living room, to where there's a couch beneath a large window that looks out on the blanket of grass outside. He gets a start and hopes he hasn't let it show. It's not Martin that's there. It's the cop! And there's a woman sitting beside him. He frowns at Jackie, but she's got two mugs in her hand and she's bringing them to the long narrow table that they're sitting behind.

'This is Detective Brady,' she says putting a mug in front of yer one. 'And this is her partner, Detective Doyle.' She places the second mug in front of yer man. It's the mug that Joey likes to drink from. Then she sits down on an armchair across from them.

'Call me Aidan,' he says.

'I'm Rose,' she says.

She's wearing faded blue jeans and a plain white T-shirt under a tight-fitting black leather jacket. Her face is friendly, round and soft, and her eyes are looking at him with concern, like she's hoping he's not upset by their sudden arrival.

'Did you not have work today?' Jackie asks him, and both visitors stare at him like his answer is important.

'No.' He would like to tell her why, but now isn't the time. He goes to the fridge, even though he's not hungry; it's just that the presence of the two cops has thrown him. What game are they playing? It's freaking him out, but he doesn't want them or Jackie to know that.

'You hungry?' his aunt asks.

'No. I had a McDonald's.'

'Ah Jesus, Joey, that shit won't fill you.'

'I'm OK. I'll have a coffee, though.'

He goes to the sink and the coffee pot beside it, feeling all annoyed about Jackie giving his mug to the cop. He pours coffee into a substitute mug and stands with his back to them stirring in sugar and milk and waiting to hear what the conversation will be about.

'Sit over here,' Jackie says. 'Detective Doyle wants to talk to us. It's important.'

Joey turns and leans against the worktop, cradling the mug in his two hands.

'I'm listening,' he says.

Jackie looks at Doyle like he's the one in charge.

'I've met Joey already today,' Doyle says, smiling at her. 'But I didn't get much of a chance to talk to him.'

Joey surveys the man, giving him a closer inspection than when he last saw him. He has a friendly face, but the eyes are an icy blue. He's wearing a friendly smile, showing off white teeth, and he's still being cool in his student sleeves. He looks like he's more into his appearance than catching criminals. No threat to anyone.

A face that says, *I'm here out of concern for your safety*. But Joey can see what's behind the mask, can see the eyes not matching the smile.

'Will you come over here, Joey, and don't be rude,' Jackie says.

Joey sighs and goes and sits on the arm of her armchair.

'Jackie's been telling us how she knows Quinlan,' Brady says, breaking the ice. 'And she's filled in a bit about how you know him too, Joey.'

'I don't know him that well,' Joey says, giving his aunt a frown. 'I've done bits and pieces for him in the past, and I've met him a couple of times out socially when my ... my stepda was working for him. But I don't know if my aunt told you – I never liked him. And neither does she.'

'Not surprised to hear that,' Doyle says, putting his coffee aside, 'not surprised at all. But look, we're just here to tell you both that we're putting a file together on him – a lot of manpower –' He looks away to his sidekick and smiles at her. 'And a lot of womanpower too, yeah?' She smiles but Joey can see the slight roll of her eyes once his attention is away from her and she's lifting her coffee mug to her lips. 'We want to take him down, Joey.'

'Yeah, go ahead! It doesn't concern me what yiz do. The sooner yiz lock him up the better.'

'But what if it concerns your stepdad?'

'What about my stepda?'

Joey's gaze goes to Jackie, but she's looking at the cop now and seems alarmed.

'This has to do with Vinnie?' she says like it's fresh news to her. 'How?'

'That's what we don't know,' Brady adds, 'but we think he's back in Dublin.'

Doyle leans forward and pushes his coffee mug to the side like he's already finished with it, though he's hardly touched it. He glances from Joey to Jackie.

'Yeah, we think he's back here and we'd like to talk to him because we think –'

'We don't have any evidence for it, though,' Brady butts in.

Doyle gives her a look that says she should be quiet now while he's doing the important bit.

'That's right, Detective Brady. We don't have any evidence, but we know from our sources – my sources in fact – that Quinlan is pretty ... let me say ... concerned that Vinnie is back. And those sources tell me that maybe it's because Vinnie's return is about some unfinished business that's going to cause trouble for Mr Quinlan.'

'Our sources could be wrong. So, we'd like to talk to Vincent, just to check it out,' Brady says, butting in again. She gives Doyle the eye, and he shrugs his shoulders like that might be true, but he knows better and she's really said enough.

'We're just curious,' she says, ignoring the shrug. 'Vincent is back, but he seems to be in hiding, and we're wondering if that has to do with Quinlan. Like maybe he's got some info on his old boss that could help us.'

She glances across to Doyle and he nods, like she's doing well but it's time for him to talk once more.

'It's strange, don't you think, that he's back here and hasn't contacted any of his family? And his presence seems to be spooking Quinlan. Could be he's got something that Quinlan doesn't want broadcast.'

Brady looks towards Jackie, like she's a lawyer appealing to a jury.

'We're just trying to make a case against Mr Quinlan and we need all the help we can get. He's a dangerous man. He's pulling in young boys, even younger than Joey there, and offering them jobs they think they can turn into careers.'

'Yeah,' Doyle butts in. 'And young boys are very vulnerable. I'm sure Joey knows that from the criminal activity his stepda pulled him into.'

'What are you talking about?' Jackie says, like she's suddenly annoyed. 'What criminal activity?'

Joey thinks he can see a glint in the cop's eyes like he's delighted with the little explosion his lobbed grenade has caused.

'Well, Vinnie disappeared before we could look into it. And it mightn't be Vinnie in the picture at all. But Joey might be able to fill in some of the details.'

'I don't know what you're talking about!' Joey snaps. 'And I don't care anymore where my stepda is living. And neither does Jackie. So, if yous want to find him yiz should get off your arses and look for him yourselves. And anyway you're wasting your time because even if he was back here, he'd want nothing to do with Quinlan. And he won't want to talk to yous two either because he's not a rat.'

The two cops look towards Jackie.

'What Vinnie does in his own time is none of our business,' Jackie says. 'And if he's back here and doesn't want to talk to me, then I'm fine with that. And if he doesn't want to talk to Joey, it seems Joey is fine with that too. We've all had our fill of Vinnie, so maybe you'll need to look elsewhere for help to bring this Mr Quinlan down.' She gets to her feet. 'And that's about all the help we can give you,' she says, making it obvious she'd like them to leave.

6

When the cops are gone, Jackie lights one of her sage-scented candles and places it on the coffee table.

'We want to bring him down! Like what TV cop show did he take that line from?'

She lifts the two mugs off the table and empties the cold coffee down the sink before sticking both in the dishwasher.

'Tosser!' Joey says, like he's answering her question. 'And why'd you give him my favourite mug? I'll never be able to drink out of it again.'

Jackie gives him a puzzled look. 'You've a favourite mug?'

'Yeah! The one you gave him.'

'That seagull one!'

'Yeah! Sharon gave it to me when I started work.'

'Well, I'm very sorry about that, Joey. You should've told me.'

'I'm telling you now. I didn't see you giving your good china cup to yer woman.'

Jackie chuckles and bangs the dishwasher door shut. 'Tosser is right! I wouldn't trust a word out of his mouth. And he knows more about what's going on than he's letting on to us, or even to that Brady woman that was with him.'

'Yeah, I felt the same,' Joey says, and he knows Jackie is waiting for more info from him but he has nothing to tell her.

'What was he on about, Joey?'

'What do you mean?'

'What was yer man Doyle referring to, about Vinnie and you and some sort of criminal activity?'

'Joyriding! And nicking stuff. Isn't that criminal enough for yeh?' Joey can't hold her gaze.

'But why did Vinnie leave here so suddenly? Why? And you're not the same since he left.'

'Is that not a good thing?'

'I think it's great, Joey. But I don't get how you've changed towards him. I thought you liked him? You used call him 'Da', as far as I remember. And the pair of ye, thick as ... whatever?'

'Yeah well, he didn't run off to Donegal because of me. He went off, as far as I know, to get work. Because Quinlan is a crook and he didn't want to be working for him any more.'

'I don't know if I can believe that, Joey. From what I know of Vinnie he never objected to working with crooks.'

Joey feels his face burn and he turns away from her. He gets to his feet and places his coffee mug in the sink, though he knows he should put it elsewhere.

'I'm doing an extra late shift so you can have this place to yourselves if you want to bring Sharon back.'

That would be nice – him and Sharon alone, like it was his own pad. But maybe he's blown it with freaking out over that cop. He shouldn't have said anything.

He checks his phone. 'Call me!' the screen shouts with a large red heart planted after the message. Fucking emojis. He hates them, most of the time. But this one he loves.

'Well?

He turns around and Jackie is still there. She's talking to him, asking him more questions about Vinnie but he's not letting them register. He sniffs the purifying aroma that's wafting towards him from off the candle and taps a thumbs-up into the phone and taps three hearts after it, then takes two of them quickly away, then subtracts the last one and presses SEND.

7

His card has four names on it.

'He was sent home from Saipan,' he says to Sharon.

'Saipan? Where the fuck is Saipan?'

'He's a Cork footballer!'

'Jack Lynch.'

'Jack Lynch, Sharon. Who the fuck is Jack Lynch?'

'The tunnel. They named the tunnel after him. In Cork.'

'What tunnel?'

'Oh, for Jesus sake do the next one, Joey. It's called "Thirty Seconds" not "Thirty Minutes".'

Miles is cracking up and spilling his beer on the IKEA round table he spent so much time telling them all about earlier. Rodney is sucking on his spliff, then taking a fit of coughing like the scene is too much for him. He's not wearing his beret, and his hair is shorn tight.

'The next one, Joey, for fucksake the next one,' she's screeching at him, and the two lads are in fits now.

He sees the name, remembers the film, the series he saw her in on the telly. 'Yer one!' She glares at him. 'Great looking chick!'

'You can't say "chick", Joey.'

'I said once you looked like her.'

'When?'

'How can I remember when – when we were watching a stupid film or series or something.'

'What film? Name the film.'

'I can't remember. You said it was great, you said she was so sexy.'

Miles and your man Rodney are nearly rolling on the floor at this stage and Sharon is all distracted looking at them.

'She's an actress – an American actress. She has a long name. She tried to commit suicide once. Not with her knife, though!'

He mimes feeding himself soup from a bowl.

'With her spoon!' Sharon shouts. 'WITHERSPOON! Reece Witherspoon!'

She's laughing out loud at him and doesn't seem to care that the timer has spilled all its sand ages ago. He hasn't got a chance to try for the last name, and it's just as well because he can't even pronounce the word let alone give her a clue.

'Hey, Shar,' Miles hoots, 'Joey gets the prize for the best clue I've ever heard.'

When the game is over, Sharon goes into her bedroom to hang clothes and he sits on the double bed and watches her. Then she's opening her laptop and arranging books and a folder of pages on her work table that the two lads bought second-hand especially for her. He knows she has an essay to work on that his presence has interrupted.

'Thanks,' she says, before he goes back out to the lads.

'For what?'

'For being good fun.'

'Am I?' he says.

'You are. And the two lads think you're funny.'

'I am funny.'

'Yeah, you can be, Joey. But don't lose the run of yourself – like, don't act the clown.'

Joey's not sure how to take this comment, so he says nothing, just frowns at her.

'You know exactly what I mean, Joey. But look, talk to me before you go. Or if it's late, get in beside me.'

'Yeah.' He smiles. That's the best offer he's had all day.

He sips a bottle of beer. It's just the third one he's had all night. It's cheap and German and strong, so he's careful now. He took two drags from the spliff and it was good stuff, but he has to work in the morning and he wants to have a clear head, plus he doesn't want to go back to that person he was before.

Miles has nodded off, his head resting on Rodney's shoulder as Rodney tries to tell Joey the type of art he's doing. He shows Joey on his phone. It's full of drawings of Miles. There are lots of trees also, and close-up photos of tree bark, with patterns that he says are reconnecting him to nature. He says he has lots of samples of his work in his bedroom but he looks kindly at Miles like it would be too cruel to deny him the pillow he's resting his head on.

Joey tells him about how Jackie got him the job in the shop. She knows the owner. But he tells him too about how pissed off he's getting with Hazel, the manager, for making him feel like he's not to be trusted. He's too friendly with the customers! What kind of screwy store policy is that? But it's the reason, he tells Rodney, why he might go back to college and do something with his life. He's just not sure yet.

'Sharon told us you're a brilliant driver,' Rodney says, and Joey grimaces. It feels like a compliment, but he's not sure if Sharon meant it as one.

'She said you did a lot of joyriding.'

'She told you that?'

'You have a bit of the James Dean thing going on.'

'That didn't end well,' Joey says, and they both smile.

Rodney grows tired of talking and Joey leaves him to tidy up and goes into Sharon's room. She's lying on the bed in a vest and shorts, showing off her long sleek athlete's legs. Her laptop is on her chest and she's fast asleep. He lifts the laptop off her and places it on her work table that's a sea of pages, with scribbled-on post-it notes stuck to them like sailing boats. She groans but doesn't wake up.

He sees where she has spread out newspaper clippings on the floor like she wants to sort them, or maybe analyse them like she's one of those whip-smart detectives he's seen on the telly. He smiles. He bends down to examine what the clippings are about. He sees the photo of a woman who was mugged on Talbot Street and he quickly reads the short article underneath that tells how she's now coping.

There's a photo of a guy in a wheelchair, and another page is telling the story of a family terrorised by a burglar. His eyes are drawn to one of the clippings that carries a short headline above the photos.

Father dies from heart attack trying to stop thieves

He can feel a shiver that causes a shudder in his shoulders, and his legs go weak. His eyes are wide and his mouth is hanging open as he picks up the page and stares at it until the words come into focus. He places a hand on the carpet so he can examine the two photos that come with the article. There's one of the man, the father, dressed in a tuxedo and looking like an Elvis impersonator. The other photo is of the dead man's wife. She's called Georgina. She has her arm around her daughter, who's called Amber. The girl looks about the same age as his half-sister, Isabel. He reads the article quickly. They've moved house because of what happened. They're out in Clontarf somewhere. It doesn't say where but the photo shows the girl outside her new school. The story gives an account of what happened. It's accurate – except they weren't trying to steal the car, just the catalytic converter. Joey closes his eyes to shut away the headline, but he can't shut off the memory that pops up now in his brain.

The man appears, like from nowhere. He's not dressed like Elvis now, he's wearing a T-shirt and blue pyjama bottoms, and shiny shoes that have the laces open. The pyjama top is flapping wide and his fat belly is pushing out his white vest. He's waving a golf iron and mouthing curses, and it looks like he's going to wallop Weso, when suddenly he grabs at his chest and lets the golf iron fall to the ground.

Vinnie slides out from beneath the car and stares at the man where he's lying on the ground. Joey takes his phone out to ring for an ambulance but the phone gets grabbed from his hand and then all he can remember is the squealing van and the woman screaming, racing from the house with the young girl sprinting behind.

'Don't mess those up on me, Joey!'

Sharon is sitting up in her bed and she's frowning at him. 'What's wrong, Joey? You're as white as a sheet.'

Joey opens his mouth but can't find words. He glances down at the page in his hand but doesn't want to draw attention to it. What's going on?

She places her two feet on the floor and stretches.

'That's all stuff to do with my big essay. I'm doing it on restorative justice in case you're wondering.'

'What?'

'Restorative justice! It's a programme for people who've been affected by crime. The victims get to meet the perpetrators and it's, like, done to help them lessen the trauma they're carrying. And it benefits the criminals too. Helps with guilt. I'm looking at people or families who've been through the process. Yeah? And I'm also looking at cases where I think it might be appropriate to do it. It's done through mediation, Joey … like I might train to be a mediator at some stage … or I could get a job in the probation service.'

'I thought you want to be a social worker?'

'This is what social work is all about, Joey.'

He shows her the article in his hand.

'This ... this is nearly a year old, Sharon. Like, why have you still got it?' He's afraid of sounding like he's accusing her of something.

'Oh ... I held on to that one because I thought ...'

'What?'

'I thought maybe ... like ... Wesley ...'

'You thought Wesley was involved?'

'I don't know. Well, yeah, because he didn't want to talk about it when it happened. It was all over the local paper. And you didn't want to talk about it either, Joey.'

He looks at the page. He's afraid to look at her. She'll see through him. She'll know he's lying. Maybe he should tell her now and get it over with. She'll finish with him but maybe it's for the best.

'I didn't want to talk about it, Sharon ... because of the man ... lying there ... dead on the ground.'

'Oh my God!' Sharon cries. She's standing now. 'Oh my God, I'm so stupid! Your poor da, lying on the floor in that bookshop. Oh my God! How could I be so stupid.'

Now he can bear to look at her.

'Yeah.' Then he looks away again.

'I won't use it, Joey. I won't. You can scrap it.'

Joey puts the page to one side of him.

'Come on to bed, Joey. It's late ... and you're upset ... and it's my fault.'

Joey sighs like he's suddenly exhausted. He is exhausted.

'I've to go to the bathroom first,' he says.

'OK!' She goes to the line-up of newspaper clippings and gathers them all up while Joey makes his escape.

'Joey!' she calls as he opens the door. He turns. 'I'm sorry for being ... short with you ... but it's just ... I'm really loving doing all this ... this studying. I never thought I'd ever say something like that. And I want to get this essay right before I let Miles read it.'

In the bathroom he sits on the toilet and stares at the newspaper clipping. They have names. That's the hardest bit for him. They have names. One is as young as Isabel, the other could be his own ma. He doesn't read the name of the man. He doesn't want to know his name. His da had a name. Ted. He finds it hard to remember his face. He can only remember seeing him lying on the floor in the kiddies' area of the bookshop in town. It looked like he was asleep – or pretending to be asleep.

He thinks about shredding the page and flushing it but he won't do that. He'll take it away with him – take it away so it can't sour her new life in the city. He sits and knows she's waiting for him. But he feels a heavy weight across his chest. He's lied to her. Though it wasn't a lie – the way he told it. It wasn't a lie. She would have been upset. He can't be upsetting her now when she's here all excited about being a student.

He's going to be a different Joey from now on. He glances at the page and then folds it and puts it out of sight in his leather wallet. Out of sight is out of mind. Isn't that what his ma says he's good at doing?

A different Joey is all he wants to be. But how can he be a different Joey if Vinnie is out there somewhere wanting to pull him back into his schemes?

8

Today Joey's on the food counter and up to his elbows in butter tubs and mayonnaise spread. The food is pretty decent and he always makes sure to plump up the rolls. He makes up his own combos or suggests stuff he thinks the customers will like. And he notices how the egg mayonnaise he makes himself is a lot tastier than the runny mess that arrives in those plastic containers. It's the spoon of French mustard he adds like Jackie taught him to do.

Being busy keeps his mind off thinking and that's the main reward from a job like this. But Vinnie's voice keeps creeping in.

'Get a grip, Joey! That man was an accident waiting to happen. Did you see the size of him? The belly on him! I bet he had loads of warnings beforehand but the dozy bastard probably wouldn't go to the doctor to get himself checked out. And he didn't heed those other warnings either, the ones you hear being given out by the cops. Like, what the fuck was he at? You never run out like that –

waving a golf stick like it's a sword and you're a one-man fuckin' cavalry. If he hadn't kicked the bucket that night then it would have been some other night shortly after. Do you hear me, Joey? So cut out the guilt shit.'

He concentrates on his work. But it isn't the kind of work that will keep Sharon with him. She's told him she expects more from him, especially if they're going to get a place of their own.

He gets his first text from her at nine.

Really sorry Joey for upsetting you.

She sends a stream of emoji crap – every second one a heart.

Joey answers:

Hey no worries.

He gets another text an hour later.:

Someone stole my laptop.

WTF

She comes back:

Someone just grabbed it from me
and ran from the college.

He calls her.
'What the fuck, Sharon?'

'Oh, Joey, what am I going to do? Everything I've done so far is on it. My essay that I'd nearly finished.'

'I'll get you a new one,' Joey says immediately.

'A new one is no good to me when my work is gone. And anyway you don't have that sort of money.'

'I've enough.'

'But you were saving for a car.'

'What do I need a car for, living where I am? Was anyone with you when it happened?'

'No. I'd just left Miles and Rodney. I think the thieves were following me once they saw the laptop.'

'You saw who they were?'

'No. Not really. They had their hoodies up and they had those electric scooters. All I could see was the back of them.'

Joey remembers the scooter head in Trinity and the two lads he saw on the street and wonders if it was any of them.

'It's nothing to do with –' she starts.

He cuts her off. 'With what? He can hear her sigh. 'I said with what?'

'Nothing!'

He knows what she's getting at but doesn't say anything. 'I'll be off by four.'

'OK. I'm going down to the Garda station to report it.'

It bothers Joey what she said – what she more than hinted at. *It's nothing to do with* ... But he's so busy he forgets about it.

He's flat-out making rolls for the lads who are building apartments round the corner. And when that dies down

Hazel has him on the till next to her and she's not bothering to talk to him.

The homeless guy who sits outside the shop door – Moses they call him – comes in with a lottery ticket that someone has given him. There's five-euro winnings on it and he heads straight for the off-licence corner to pick out his prize. And after that Bridie from the flats across the street is in and she's buying her smokes and hands him a Lotto ticket and asks him to check the numbers. And when he does, he sees she's won fifty euro and, just for a second, he's on the verge of telling her hard luck and does she want her ticket back or will he bin it – but he pushes those thoughts down and smiles at her and tells her it's her lucky day and hands her the fifty, and he knows from the way she stares at the note that she hasn't seen one of them any time recently.

And then a young fella glides in the door on his scooter and heads straight towards Joey. He's wearing new black Nike Air Max runners and grey tracksuit-bottoms, with a grey hoodie beneath a smart looking sleeveless black puffer jacket. He could be one of the lads he's spotted earlier, though the runners are different to the Vans the other lads were wearing. He's got a black computer bag strapped around his shoulder, like maybe he's some sort of weird postman doing his rounds. He halts in front of Joey and the hood is up and his head is sunk into it, so Joey can only see the pale mask of a face and the cold empty eyes. Hazel's mouth hangs open at the sheer audacity of the boy. Joey puts his hand out to touch her sleeve, to let her know he'll deal with it. The eyes are staring at Joey and Joey knows he's not here to buy anything.

'You can't bring that yoke in here,' Joey says to him.

The boy – he's only about twelve – doesn't seem to notice what Joey has said, or if he does, he really doesn't care. He opens the computer bag and takes out a laptop. He turns it over so Joey can see both sides of it and see it's got Sharon's name and phone number on the sticker she attached to the back of it. He places the laptop on the counter and then he turns and glides out of the shop.

'What the hell!' Hazel says. 'Is he a friend of yours?' She leans in to see the laptop. 'What's he giving you that for?'

'It's Sharon's,' he says. 'It was stolen from her just this morning.'

'And that lad is bringing it back? Do you know him?' She says it like it's an accusation.

Joey shrugs. 'I don't know who he is or how he knew to bring it in here. I don't know what's going on.'

Hazel shakes her head. 'Next time, you tell him he's not to come in here on one of those yokes.'

'I told him,' Joey says, and there's a new customer in front of him waiting for attention so he can't continue the conversation with Hazel – not that he wants to. A few minutes later he's got time to inspect the laptop for any sign of damage. But what the hell is going on? Who is this little toerag who has obviously stolen it on her and brought it back?

The shop is quiet and Hazel sends him to do a bit of shelf packing. He takes the laptop from beneath the counter and is on his way to the store room to get a box of Hobnobs when he spots Weso. He's inside the door scanning the shop for a sign of Joey. Joey wants to duck but is too slow, and Weso sees him and heads towards him.

'What's going on, Weso?'

'What do yeh mean?'

'You know what I mean! You, working for Quinlan. And what's with this new white shirt and waistcoat, like you're a choir boy?'

'That's Quinlan's doing. Says if I want to be driving his car, I can't be looking like I stole the fuckin' thing. The fucker won't let me wear shades, though. What's that about?'

'I don't know, Weso, but what's with you blanking me like you never met me before in your life?'

'Look, I had to do it that way, Joey. Don't you know Quinlan was testing me just as much as he was fuckin' with your head? Anyway, who else can guarantee me safety from Ginsey McGinn and his loopy crew? Or guarantee my ma's safety either? She's out there every day on her bike delivering the post.'

He sees Hazel glancing over at the pair of them and he knows she's wondering what the hell is going on – like maybe he's helping Weso rob stuff on her.

'Were you with Vinnie when they did the job on Ginsey?' Joey asks.

'Yeah. I just drove, though.'

'I asked you before and you pretended not to know much about it.'

'Yeah, but that was just to protect you in case the cops came asking you questions.'

'For fucksake, Weso!'

'Fucksake nothing! I enjoyed every minute of what Vinnie did to Ginsey. The rat. But you saw him for yourself there. He's frothing at the mouth, itching for revenge.'

'You think Quinlan's going to protect you?'

'For the moment – or at least until I think of a better plan.'

'Have you seen this?' Joey says, showing him the sticker.

'It's Sharon's, so what?'

'Some little scumbag stole it on her this morning and then he glides in here on his electric scooter like he owns the place and just hands it to me without a word of explanation.'

'So that's what this is about.'

'What?'

'Quinlan told me to come down here and give you a message.'

'What message?'

'He said he wants back what Vinnie stole from him.'

'Vinnie? What did he steal from Quinlan?'

'The car he went off in when he left Dublin. And there was a laptop in the boot too that he wants.'

'I thought that was Vinnie's own car?'

'Half of it was. He still owed Quinlan for the other half.'

'So why did he have Sharon's laptop taken and then give it back to me? Like, what's that about?'

'I dunno! I suppose it's to say Vinnie took things belonging to him and he's going to do the same to you. Or if not to you, then to the people you care about.'

'Fucksake, Weso!'

'Don't you know this is the way Quinlan operates? Did you not hear him, the way he talked to you in the car? It's like every conversation you have with that guy feels like some sort of threat. He plays games with your head, Joey. Amuses himself, letting you know he can get at you any time he likes. I made the mistake of telling him about Sharon going to college and about how much she loves being a student. So, what does he do with that bit of info? The fucker uses it to let the two of us know he can ruin everything on her if you don't get him what he wants. And he has those little toerags buzzing around him like flies around shite and falling over each other to be his best boy.'

'Those scooter heads?' Joey asks.

'Yeah. Quinlan's like yer man with the ugly bull-dog – yer man in that Oliver Twist film that mad yoke of a teacher showed us when we were at school. And they're queueing up to join him. He buys them the scooters and gives them a fancy computer bag to carry their gear in.'

'So, this is all about Vinnie and what he took? The car, like, and the computer?'

'Yeah. Half the car. And now Quinlan's wondering why Vinnie's come back but hasn't come near him. He thinks your stepda is hiding away because he's up to something. And someone's got in his ear especially about that laptop. I don't know what's going on, but Quinlan's really spooked.'

'I don't believe that, Weso. There has to be a different reason Vinnie's here. It doesn't have to mean he's going back to his old ways.'

'What? He's had a brain transplant?'

'Not funny, Weso,' Joey says, feeling himself getting annoyed.

'Yeah, but you need to remember that all those fuckers like Quinlan are paranoid. Quinlan and his lot think everyone is out to get them. You even disagree with him about the weather and he'll be eyeing you like he wants to strip search you for a wire or something.'

Joey lowers his eyes and scans the shop once more. There's a guy over near the door doing the Lotto and a young couple in the off-licence section messing up his beer display. And Hazel is at the counter, frowning, and watching Weso like maybe the robbery is going to take place immediately and she should call the cops.

'But couldn't Vinnie be back because he wants to be here? Like, I know he doesn't give a shite any more about me. But he might want to be close to Isabel.'

'If you're stupid enough to believe that, go ahead. But I don't. Vinnie's always working some angle.'

Joey has no real answer because maybe it's true.

'So, you're saying I've to find Vinnie and get him to give back the car and the laptop and whatever else he has belonging to Quinlan?'

'Yeah, Joey, or else Sharon won't have the life she wants in college. That's what that thing about stealing her laptop and then giving it back was about. And you know who she'll blame if that happens.'

'Yeah.'

Joey sighs, knowing exactly what's in store for him if he doesn't find Vinnie. But if the cops can't find him and Quinlan doesn't know where he is, then how is Joey supposed to get to him?

9

Joey texts Isabel to tell her he's on his way, then takes the red Luas round the corner from his place and heads out of town.

When he gets off, he stands on the platform and pulls the baseball cap tight around his head and then lifts the hoodie up to conceal his face. He's wearing the new knee-length raincoat that Sharon made him buy out of his first wages. It's from one of those Italian clothes shops with a fancy Italian name. She says it's only gorgeous on him. He could be mistaken for an Italian, and what the fuck does it matter, she says, if it doesn't keep the rain off? He knows he's spoiling the effect with the baseball cap but Sharon isn't here to give him fashion advice.

Once out the entrance gate he spies his sister near the pedestrian lights talking to some lad he doesn't recognise. The lad has an electric scooter. 'Fucksake!' he says to himself.

'Oi! Isabel!' he shouts.

Isabel seems to forget about the lad and walks to meet him. She stops in front of him and smiles like she's really pleased to see him. She looks smart in her school uniform.

'I LOVE the coat, Joey! Sharon'll have you on a catwalk if you're not careful.'

She smirks as she fingers the navy material. Joey has his two eyes on the lad who is watching.

'Who's that guy?' Joey says, like he's a cop. 'And I didn't want you to come down and meet me.'

He wants to hug her but doesn't know where this feeling has sprung from, and anyway he shouldn't do it in case he embarrasses her – though to be honest she doesn't embarrass easily. There's too much of Vinnie in her blood.

'That's just Mikey. He's from my school. He's in sixth class but everyone thinks he's in secondary.'

'Mikey who?'

'Mikey none of your business, Joey,' she says and giggles. She turns and calls to the lad.

'Hey, Mikey, come and meet my Italian brother.'

The lad wheels the scooter towards them and Joey is relieved somewhat to see he's wearing a school uniform – though his jumper is green and not black like Isabel's one.

'This is the Joey I was telling you about,' she says, by way of introduction.

Joey smiles at the lad. He's a little taller than his sister with the same colour brown hair and the same brown eyes. He has a brainy-looking head on him. That's another good sign to go along with the uniform.

'He's my friend,' she says, like she knows what Joey is thinking.

'Nice to meet you, Mikey,' he says. 'Friends, yeah!'

Mikey's face goes red. No danger that Isabel's would.

Joey laughs. It's the first time he's laughed all day and he's glad his sister has a friend who is different to Weso and those other scooter heads from town.

He has a sneaky look at her as they turn and head for the house. Is she in fifth class or sixth? He can't remember. But she's growing like she's already a teenager and taken on a different body shape that she's trying to fit into. And the only problem is she's starting to look a lot more like her da than her ma. He smiles at her.

'What?' she says.

'Nothing!' He can't believe how pleased he is to see her.

The road is quiet outside the house.

'Is Ma home?' Joey asks.

'Yeah. She's probably out the back – smoking.'

'She's not the only one who smokes,' Mikey says.

'I thought you had to go home,' Isabel says to him.

'I do. I am.' He steps forward like he might give her a hug but then seems to change his mind, or else he's picked up the vibe coming off her. He turns abruptly and scoots off without another word. Joey laughs out loud.

'He's a fuckin' pest,' Isabel says but Joey knows she's lying.

They go in the door and he calls out but there doesn't seem to be anyone about. He goes into the kitchen and now he can see his ma sitting in the back garden in the late evening sun. She's drinking a mug of tea and smoking and at the same time scrolling through her phone.

As soon as she spots him, she's up from her chair to grab hold of him. She takes him in her arms and holds him tight. Then she pushes him away from her so she can have a good look at him. It feels like he's ten.

'My God, Joey, you look just great.' She turns to Isabel, who has followed him out. 'Doesn't he look great?' she says.

Isabel shrugs. 'I thought you said you were angry with him. He didn't come out for my birthday or his da's anniversary.'

'Do I stay angry with you, Isabel, when you upset me?' Ma says.

Isabel sniffs but seems happy enough to have made her point.

'You're still smoking, Ma,' Joey says.

'Yeah, she is,' Isabel adds, and Ma gives her the evil eye.

'Yeah, but at least now I do it outside.'

'Oh wow!' Isabel says, as she moves away from them and heads indoors.

'That one would give you a pain in the hole,' Ma says as she puts her phone on the table and sits back like she wants to relax with her smoke while she admires Joey some more. It's the coat. Then she sighs as she spies the yellow lamp light come on in Isabel's room.

'I'm sorry I wasn't here for Da's anniversary,' says Joey.

'So where were you?'

'I had to work.'

'Could you not get the time off, then?'

'I could, but I … I never asked. I'm sorry, Ma.'

'For God's sake, Joey!'

'What?'

'It wasn't your fault.'

'What wasn't?'

'It wasn't your fault he died!'

'I know!'

'It was a brain haemorrhage.'

'I know!'

'So why couldn't you be here for the anniversary, then?'

'Oh look, Ma ...'

'It wasn't your fault!'

She takes a drag of the smoke. Flakes of ash fall away into her lap and she tries to brush them off her jeans with a back flick of her fingers but only manages to paint them in.

'I know it wasn't my fault, Ma, but I feel bad sometimes ... like, he was in there buying a book for me, when he could have been at home. And if he was home maybe then ...'

'It would've happened no matter where he was, Joey. Besides, he wasn't just in there buying a book for you. He was in town mainly to buy a fishing reel for himself.'

'I know, ma, but sometimes I think I was a real whingy child. A bit of a head-melt!'

'For fucksake, Joey, you were a sweet little boy that your da liked to spoil. That's who you were.' There's a small shake in her voice and he can see her eyes moist over.

She finishes her cigarette and stubs it out in the cracked cereal bowl she uses as her ashtray. She sniffs and rubs at her nose with the back of her hand.

He was only four when it happened. He remembers the cover of the book his da bought him. He remembers his da reading it to him. It was one of those books with flaps with little animals hiding behind each one that the dog was searching for. He doesn't know what happened to the book. Maybe it got left behind in the shop. He can't remember anything else that happened that day – just the book, and his da, with his head lying on the arms of his denim jacket. But he's not going to try remembering stuff now.

They sit quietly and it feels like his ma is waiting for him to say something more about his da. But he's not going to do that.

'You need to have a word with her,' Joey says instead, raising his eyes towards Isabel's room.

'Who? Isabel?'

'Yeah. You need to tell her stuff about ... you know ... '

'What?'

'You know! Her and this Mikey bloke. He looks years older than her.'

His ma laughs. 'For God's sake, Joey, they're just friends. They go to the library together. He's teaching her how to play chess.'

'Maybe she's teaching him a few moves too, Ma. She's not as innocent as she looks.'

'Who are yeh telling!' She laughs once more. 'Maybe you should stick around, Joey, and try and have that talk with her yourself.'

She takes a packet of cigarettes from her cardigan and lights one up. She inhales the smoke, then blows it out up towards the sky.

'Vinnie's back and everyone's crying wolf,' Joey says.

Joey's ma lowers her cigarette and hides her eyes.

'You know?' Joey says.

'Yeah, I figured he was somewhere about.'

'How?'

'A present got dropped off here for her ladyship. It was left in the porch. I just figured it was him. How did you find out?'

'Quinlan told me.'

'Quinlan?'

'Yeah.'

'What's Quinlan got to do with him?'

'Ma, I don't know. But Quinlan says Vinnie's back in Dublin and he's mad keen to talk to him.'

'To give him his job back?'

'For God's sake, Ma. He thinks Vinnie is back in order to cause him trouble.'

'What kind of trouble?'

'I don't know. But if Quinlan calls here asking about him, you make sure to say it's the first you've heard of it.'

'Oh my God. Did you tell Isabel?'

'No.'

'Well don't. I told her the present got dropped by a courier. If she gets wind he's here she'll want him back in her life again and I don't want that to happen.'

His ma takes another pull on her smoke. She inhales it deep into her chest, then sighs it all back out again. Joey gets to his feet.

'What the hell happened, Joey?'

'What do you mean?'

'You know what I'm talking about. You and him were as thick as thieves. And then you tell me you want nothing more to do with him, like he's the devil himself. And he disappears in a flash, leaving me to deal with Isabel. She accused me of driving him out of the city – said was I not happy enough that I'd driven him out of her house?'

She eyes Joey, waiting for his explanation, but he has none he wants to offer her. 'Something must have happened that you're not telling me about.'

'Nothing happened. I just wised up, that's all.'

'Well, I'm glad to hear that, Joey. I'm really glad. Now if that one upstairs would only wise up about him also.'

Joey goes to move away from the table.

'You're not going already?'

'I'm just going up to chat to her for a while and then I'll go.'

His ma takes another drag on the smoke and now her mind seems elsewhere. Joey knows where she's gone off to. He stops at the back door and looks back at her. She has her phone to her ear and he knows she's calling Jackie.

10

Isabel is sitting at her study table. She's got her school books in a neat pile to one side so she has space for the plastic chess set full of black and white pieces she's now peering down at. On the other side of the table is her laptop. Beside it is a small cardboard box that sits in torn wrapping paper. There's a collection of sloppy pink birthday cards on the shelf just above the desk and they're fighting for space among her photos that show her in different poses with her da, like she's an only child. Joey hasn't got a card for her, though it's a bit late now. He totally forgot her birthday.

She eyes him suspiciously as he takes up a framed photo that's behind the laptop. She's with a group of lads and girls and they're all making mad looking poses for the camera like they're trees. He spots the lad Mikey.

She takes the photo off him and places it carefully back on the table.

'That's my drama group.'

'I see your man Mikey there.'

'So?'

'So I didn't know you were into drama.'

She groans loudly so he turns away from her to admire her room.

There's new carpet on the floor that's a dark colour, and the quilt on the bed is top half white and bottom half black. There are new yellow curtains hanging, and the walls are freshly painted.

'Powder blue!' she says and laughs when she sees how impressed looking he is. 'And the carpet is midnight navy.'

'Did your da pay for all that?'

'Yeah. And Ma didn't even want me to have it. Like she doesn't want me to have nice things. And see what else Da got me.' She nods at the crumpled wrapping paper. Joey moves to her side and opens the lid. There's a small square of black plastic that's the size of the wall tile that Joey's Ma uses to put her teapot on. There are letters in white written on the black plastic and there's a wire with plug attached coiled neatly beside the box.

Joey recognises it immediately because Weso got one of them for his ma.

'A dodgy box! Yeah?'

'Yeah, but Ma won't let me use it on the telly, even though we could watch every programme and every film ever made. We could watch everything! She said it's illegal! She's only saying that because my da bought it for me and she doesn't want me to be happy.'

'It is illegal,' Joey says, trying to defend his ma.

'Not really. The person selling them can get in trouble. But not the person using them. That's what my da said.'

'You're talking to your da?'

'On the phone.'

'On the phone?'

'Is there something wrong with your hearing, Joey? That's what I said. He calls me every week to check in with me.'

'Where does he call you from?'

'I don't know. Different places. I'm not the cops, Joey.'

'That's nice … that he's calling you.'

Joey doesn't believe it's nice.

'Yeah and it's more than you do.'

He goes to sit on the end of her bed. She places the dodgy box back in its wrapping and puts it in the drawer of her desk.

'I asked him was he selling them and he said he wasn't.'

'Well, that's definitely true so,' Joey says.

'Don't you annoy me, Joey. And how come you get to live with Aunt Jackie and I can't?'

Joey lets out a loud sigh. Maybe he should tell her the truth about her da. Maybe he could get her to watch the CCTV video on YouTube and then she might see him in a different light. But she wouldn't believe it.

'My ma hates me,' she says. 'And she doesn't like Mikey either. I know she doesn't. I wish my da was here.'

He should tell her everything. Then she wouldn't want her da back ever again. But if he tells, he'll have to let her know about his part in it. He can't bear to do that; can't bear the thought of how she might look at him.

'She hates him too,' she goes on. 'He could be lying dead in a ditch or on the side of a street somewhere for all she cares.'

'All right!' Joey cries out. Then says quickly, 'All right,' in a lower voice.

'What's wrong?'

Joey looks away from her and rubs at his face with his hands.

'Oh my God, I'm sorry, Joey. I'm really sorry.'

He glances up at her as she moves from her chair and comes to him.

'I'm after making you think of your own poor da! Oh my God! I'm so sorry, Joey!'

She starts to bawl and goes quickly back to her chair and leans in on her table and knocks over all the chess pieces.

'I am so stupid!' she wails.

'You're not stupid,' Joey says and stands up. 'You're not stupid. You're just sad. You're just sad your own da is gone.'

He stands looking down at her black jumper and at her shoulders the way they're shuddering like she's cold. He feels helpless. He steps back from her and nearly tramples on two of the chess pieces that are littering the floor.

'I'll get Ma,' he says and leaves her to her sobbing.

11

He gets a text from Sharon as he leaves the house. She says she might be in bed by the time he calls, but there will be someone up and there's probably a few extra heads visiting – some arty-farty friends of Rodney's. He texts back that he's on his way, getting the last Luas, and inserts an emoji of a galloping horse.

The night is chilly and he pulls his coat tight around him and pulls the collar up around his neck. These coats may be grand to wear in Milan or some other Italian city but here they're fuck-all use against the cold – as well as the rain.

He doesn't notice the three hooded figures until they materialise out from the side wall of the community centre. The one out front has a crutch. He can see the shape of it.

They line out in front of him. Ginsey removes his hood – like what does he need a hood on his head for? Obvious who he is. The other two lads keep their hoods up so he doesn't know who they are. But it doesn't matter now where they're from. He knows there will be a problem getting the last Luas – or any Luas for that matter. But he's not surprised, like he wasn't surprised with the arrival that time of Quinlan's car.

'Visiting your ma, were yeh?' Ginsey calls to him as he moves sideways onto the grass margin to block Joey's attempt to cut round the three of them.

'What's it to you?' is all Joey can think of saying. He knows his tone will make things worse for him, but he knows Ginsey too long to try to be any other way with him. Once a scumbag always a scumbag.

'Your row isn't with me, Ginsey. It's with me stepda!'

'Yeah but you're here now so you'll do for starters.'

The three of them make a semi-circle round him. He looks for any sign of a weapon in their hands but they aren't carrying. There's only Ginsey's crutch. Joey scans the ground for a stone or a stick, but there's nothing. He takes off his belt and wraps it round his fist with the buckle showing. Behind them he hears the trundle of the oncoming Luas and the bell rings out like maybe it's warning people not to get off. It slides to a halt. Ginsey keeps his eyes on Joey, as the two lads check the tram for any alighting passengers. The doors don't open. Nobody exits. The tram bell rings. The Luas goes smoothly on its way.

'Look, I was a different person then, Ginsey. I don't have anything to do with my stepda any more.'

Ginsey laughs out loud and spits on the ground, then points the end of his crutch at Joey.

'Hey lads, he's a good boy now – a mammy's boy like his specky-four-eyed little sister.'

'You go near my sister or my ma and I'll fucking kill you – and if you weren't such a coward, you'd meet me here on your own.' He dangles the buckle towards the tallest of the hoods and takes a step towards them like to test the water. They don't step back. They're in no hurry. This isn't going to end well for him and he shivers. And Vinnie has caused this to happen – like Vinnie has caused all the bad stuff in his life to happen.

But it's his own fault too and maybe he deserves the beating he's going to get. Maybe it's due to him. Maybe he needs to know what it's like to have to use two crutches. Maybe he needs to know what it's like to lie panting scared on the ground. He has it coming to him, as his ma might say.

'Wait!' he shouts out towards the three lads who have circled him in. He drops the belt on the ground and puts his two hands up like he wants to surrender.

'OK! Do what you want to me. It's what I deserve. OK, Ginsey! I don't care what you do to me, just go ahead and get it over with.'

The three of them step cautiously closer, like they're not sure if Joey is up to something. But he just lowers his hands by his side and waits for the punishment.

The noise of a motorbike suddenly cuts the quiet and makes everyone freeze. Joey hopes it's a cop bike coming to save him. But there's no flashing light; there's only the front lamp that blinds them all as the bike stops. They continue to stare at it. They don't know who's riding it. Ginsey shields his eyes and moves to the side to try and get a look. They can all see the dark outline of the rider in his leathers with the round bullet head of a helmet.

The light stays on as the bike is revved up and then it's moving again and coming towards them. The lads aren't sure what to do as the bike halts once more and the driver revs the engine louder, like he's a bull and he's making ready to charge. Then they see something in the rider's hand. Joey's not sure what it is. It could be a stick. It looks like a short sword. It can't be that. He stares at it once more, and it looks like one of those telescopic truncheons some of the cops have.

The bike revs louder again and then it's driven towards them at speed. Joey moves quickly out of the way, though it never looked like it was aimed in his direction. The two hooded lads are suddenly not interested in Joey and decide to turn and run for it. Ginsey is of a similar mind, but he can only hobble. He trips over and falls and rolls onto the road, landing heavily on his shoulder. The bike is driven at him, but stops with the wheel pressed in between his two legs that are wide apart. Joey stares at the rider but there is absolutely no way of knowing who is behind the black visor.

Ginsey cries out in fear as the wheel of the bike brushes against his crotch like it's going to crush his valuables. The bike revs once more and Joey sees the dark patch on Ginsey's jeans where he's suddenly pissing himself. Joey goes towards him and the bike.

'Hey!' he shouts at the rider. 'Isn't he fucked up enough?' The helmet turns towards him but no voice is heard. The rider slowly reverses, then uses his booted feet to push the bike further out of the way. Joey goes to where Ginsey lies snivelling and bends to speak close to his ear.

'This is nothing to do with me. I don't know who this guy is. Now, get the fuck home out of here before something bad happens to yeh.'

Ginsey struggles to his feet and Joey lifts the crutch off the path and gives it to him. Ginsey doesn't look at him or say thanks but grabs the crutch and uses it to hobble off. He doesn't look back.

The bike engine is cut and the rider removes his helmet. Joey can see only long hair and a beard like Jesus might have worn. But the man is no Jesus.

It's Vinnie.

He doesn't know what to do. The grateful part of him wants to rush towards Vinnie and swamp him in a hug. But he's not going to do that.

'Howya, bud! C'mere and let me give yeh a hug.' He's standing there with his arms out like Jesus.

'I don't want a hug. I'm not a fuckin' child.'

'Oh, it's like that then, is it?'

'It's not like anything. And what are yeh doing here anyway?'

'Saving your ass is what I'm doing.'

'Yeah, well I didn't need yeh! I coulda taken them myself.'

Vinnie sniggers. 'Yeah, I can see that. Your trousers down around your arse. You were gonna shock them with the state of your jocks, were yeh?'

Joey quickly retrieves his belt and loops it back into place. He looks towards the Luas stop then back in the direction of his own house.

'I'm going home, OK?'

'Not going back into town, then?'

Joey opens his mouth, but no words escape. Vinnie laughs.

'Are you following me?' Joey asks.

'You're not that fuckin' interesting, Joey.'

'What are yeh doing here, Vinnie? And on a bike? Like, when did you start with bikes?'

Vinnie pats the bike like it's a horse.

'I like to mosey out this way on my little beast to keep an eye on things.'

'You bought it?'

'Yeah. But it's not my style, so it's up for sale if you want to buy.'

'No thanks.'

'You changed your phone number?'

'Yeah.'

'Don't want me in your life any more? Is that what it's come to?'

Joey shrugs.

'What the hell have you done to your hair, and what the fuck kind of coat is that you're wearing?' Vinnie asks, like he needs to change the subject.

'Fuckin' Sharon,' Joey says and lets slip a smile. 'But look who's talking. You look like you want to be a Hell's Angel when you're not raising the dead.'

'Yeah,' Vinnie says, patting his leather chest. Then he stares at Joey and shakes his head. 'It's good to see you, bud.'

'Yeah.'

They go silent, though both know they shouldn't be hanging round here, making small talk.

'You mean you actually drive up here every night?'

'Most nights. Just keeping an eye on things. Your ma seeing anyone this weather?'

'Not that I know of.'

'But you wouldn't tell me anyway, would yeh?'

Joey shrugs once more. He definitely wouldn't, for fear what Vinnie might do to the guy.

'Quinlan knows you're back,' Joey says, 'and he's looking for you. You need to go and talk to him. See what it's about.'

'Quinlan? What does he want with me? I never want to see that bastard again.'

'He says you stole half the car you drove off in.'

'That pile of junk.'

'Yeah. He wants it back and everything that was in it.'

'Well, I sold that piece of crap, so he can forget about it.'

Joey is supposed to tell him there's two cops looking for him, but he's not going to say anything about them because he knows Vinnie is no rat and the cops are wasting their time trying to get him to help bring Quinlan down.

'But you should go and talk to him, Vinnie. Let him know that. Straighten things out.'

'Yeah, yeah!'

'You will?'

'I said I will. OK?'

'OK. And Ma knows you're back.'

'How?'

'The present you dropped off for Isabel. She presumed it was you that did it in person. I wouldn't go near her, if I were you, Vinnie. She doesn't want anything more to do with you.'

'I know, Joey. I know. I had my chance and blew it. Yeah?'

Joey nods. 'Are you selling dodgy boxes?'

'Fucksake, yeah, Joey,' Vinnie says like he's been injected with a sudden buzz of energy. 'I'm gonna make an absolute bomb. There's a guy in Leitrim I'm getting them off. I haven't worked out the details with him yet, but I think he might want me to cover the Leinster area for him. You want a bit of the action, Joey? Hey, you interested? At least it'd be better than stacking shelves for a living.'

'I do more than stack shelves. And anyways how do you know what I'm doing?'

Vinnie taps his nose and laughs. 'Now, do you need that lift?'

'Into town?'

'I'm going that way. Or you can come out and stay with me for the night if you'd like.'

'No thanks.' Joey doesn't want to know where Vinnie lives. It's better that he doesn't know because then he doesn't have to lie in case Quinlan or the cops come bothering him again. He stares at the bike and then at Vinnie.

'I don't have a helmet.'

'You can have mine if you're afraid I'm gonna crash.'

'Keep your helmet but don't drive fast.'

'Fucksake, Joey, what's happened to you?'

'You know exactly what happened. How could I ever be the same again?'

Vinnie has no answer to that. He swipes hair away from both sides of his forehead with the back of his gloved hand, like he's rubbing away his own memories of what they did. Then he pushes his helmet back on and kicks the bike into life.

Joey doesn't know which part of Vinnie to hold onto. He's not going to put his arm around him, so he just tightens his knees against the side of the bike and holds the back of Vinnie's leather belt.

There's no way Vinnie's back to make trouble for anyone. He's just interested in selling dodgy boxes. Everyone needs to chill. And once Vinnie goes and talks to Quinlan, then everything will be OK once more.

Then he thinks about the laptop that was supposed to be in the car that Vinnie left in. Weso made it sound like Quinlan was desperate to get it back. But that's just Weso. Always the drama queen. Vinnie's probably sold that as well. He can sort it all out with Quinlan when he meets him.

Now he just wants to get to Sharon's place and let his head rest on her shoulder and close his eyes and forget all about Vinnie and his dodgy boxes and all the other dodgy plans he might be cooking up. What worries him most, though, was how good it felt to see Vinnie again, and how warm it felt to be called 'bud' once more.

12

He doesn't have a key so he waits on her step while he figures out if it's worthwhile going in to see her so late, especially when his mind is flying after the incident with Ginsey and the arrival of Vinnie. He got such a buzz when he saw his stepda standing there. But he's glad he kept his cool because it's still the same old Vinnie. He can't have changed much if he's trying to wheel and deal like the Vinnie of old. He's just about to ring the bell when he hears footsteps behind him.

'Hey there, cool guy.'

He turns and sees Rodney – and there's a girl with him, who's wearing a purple hat with a red band on it like something he's seen in the vintage shops Sharon keeps wanting to bring him to. He remembers the name of it. It's a fedora and she's added a fluffy black feather as if it wasn't loud enough already. She's wearing a black jacket that's covered in gold buttons like it could be old fancy military. He knows he's staring at it all but maybe it's to distract him from staring at her because she's a stunner, with a mop of soft brick-red curls spilling onto her shoulders, and a pair of lips like ... voluptuous, is what he thinks. Sharon would be proud of him coming up with a word like that – though maybe she wouldn't. Rodney laughs.

'Say hello to Joey, Bernice,' Rodney says.

She holds out her hand like she's the queen. She's wearing fingerless gloves. What the fuck is that about? Maybe she rides a bike. But he doesn't want to seem rude, so he shakes her hand and gives her his best smile.

'You look everything they said you were,' she says, and she's from Cork too, though it must be a different part of Cork because she sounds posher than Rodney.

Rodney has the door open and now Joey can hear something like jazz music from above. He follows the pair up the stairs and they go into Rodney's apartment and the jazz piano sounds are chilling the room and there's two lads on chairs with a girl sitting opposite them on a couch. The lads have nerdy heads on them and they've got sticks or something balanced on their knees and they look up at him and he can see it's Scrabble they're playing. What the fuck!

He's introduced to them. The lads are called Mark and Zach like they've fallen out of a bible, and the girl goes by the name of Tina. The two lads don't show much of an interest in him; they're more concerned with the game. But Tina gives him a full-on look of approval and gets to her feet and holds out her long fingers decorated with yellow nail varnish. There's a blue teapot on the front of her white

T-shirt and it's pouring a swarm of 'T' letters out of its spout. He smiles at it, and then up at her angelic-looking face and at the black hair piled up in a tower on her head and held there with the sort of large clip that Sharon used to use sometimes before she got her hair cut. There are wisps of hair hanging down to just below her ears with silver earrings dangling like Christmas decorations.

'Nice,' he says. 'Your ears!'

'My ears?'

'I mean … your earrings.'

She raises a hand to her right ear and caresses the silver like she's polishing it with her fingers.

'Did you make them yourself?' asks Joey.

'Do they look homemade?'

'No.'

'That's good. Do you like them, then?'

'Yeah, they're … gorgeous.' He can feel his face going red. He meant to say 'nice' once more, but Sharon has told him he's going to wear the word out and he needs to challenge himself and come up with some other words besides 'nice' and 'thing' and 'yoke'. 'They look like upside-down question marks.'

'You get that?' she says, beaming him a smile like he's the only one that does, and he has to look away and remember there's other people in the room. She gives him a wink and turns away and tells the lads she's had enough of the game and they place all their pieces down carefully on the table like they're only delighted to obey her.

But there's no sign of Sharon. He presumes she's in her room, but he doesn't want to be rude and go in there like he's not interested in talking to any of them. And now the lads are up off their feet and shaking his hand, saying they're delighted to meet him, and he feels like maybe he's meant to be better entertainment than their Scrabble game. Rodney shoves a beer towards him and he just takes it and sits on a stool over by the island that separates the kitchen from the sitting room. He drinks half the bottle in one gulp and realises now that his hand is shaking.

'What do you think, Bernice?' Rodney says and nods towards Joey. She steps closer and looks him up and down like maybe he's a horse she's thinking of buying. At least she doesn't squeeze his lips apart to have a look at his teeth. She smiles and turns to Rodney.

'Perfect. He's just perfect,' she says, and she goes back to Rodney and clinks her bottle off Rodney's like the deal has been sealed.

'What the fuck?' Joey says.

Rodney laughs and the other three heads are staring at him.

'You have the honour of being chosen by Bernice,' Tina says.

'Yeah?'

'Absolutely.'

Bernice scowls at her and Joey feels a bit of tension like there's some sort of bad chemistry or history between the pair of them.

Joey is staring at Bernice, at the wine-red lips, the curls flowing from the hat, and the green eyes like she's out of a commercial for chocolate, or one of those other ads that would make you want to drink coffee even if you couldn't stand the stuff.

Zach – who is scarecrow-tall and skinny, with black glasses and a crew cut head on him and with a yellow waistcoat over a white T-shirt – comes over to them and he's lugging what looks like a coat, though it could be the pelt from a baby elephant. He carefully transfers it to Bernice, who takes it and holds it open like she wants Joey to try it on.

'You want me to wear – that?' Joey says with the top of the bottle stalled just below his lips. It's a long grey leather coat with a multitude of black leather pockets. There's even some on the sleeves. It has a wide leather collar with black leather buttons down the front that have little black leather laces hanging from them.

'Yes,' Bernice says. 'Please.'

It's the way she says the please that melts his resistance. He places the bottle on the table top and turns his back to the coat and spreads his arms wide.

She pulls the coat around him and then she stands back to have a look at it. It's then that Sharon comes noisily in the door with Miles in her wake and laughing at something he's just said.

'OH, MY GAWD!' Sharon howls when she sees Joey. 'OH MY GAWWWD, Bernice, that is just soooo amaaaazing looking.'

'Do you think so?' Bernice says, and all the rest of them join in with their howls of approval – except maybe for Tina, who is busy adjusting one of her question marks.

Joey grins stupidly at Sharon. He knows from the shine in her eyes that she's tipsy – even more than tipsy, but what the hell. And maybe the way her eyes lit up was because of the coat and not him inside it but he doesn't care.

'I told you, Bernice. I told you he'd be perfect for the gig.'

'What gig?' Joey says.

'Bernice is doing fashion design in college. They're putting on a little bit of a show for some of the local design shops. You, Joey, are going to model her men's fashion range.'

'Fuck off!' is all Joey can say, and that makes everyone laugh, especially Tina. 'I mean it! No fucking way.'

Bernice makes a pout at him with those lips of hers, and he has to quickly turn away from her. Sharon goes to him and throws her arms around his waist, then peers up at him lovingly with her drink-sparkle eyes.

'And anyways … nobody need never know Bad-Ass Joey did it,' she playfully whispers, so loud they can all hear. She nibbles at his ear, hiccups into it, then pulls away from him and puts out her hand like she's introducing him. 'Hello yiz all. This is me fella – Joey Cool. Me fella dat looks like yer man … yer man with the porch.' She's much drunker than Joey realised. And they all laugh as Sharon takes the bottle of beer that Miles points at her and raises it in a toast to the whole room. Bernice is taking photos of her and of him and he's not sure if Sharon will want to see them. But they all have their phones out and are snapping away – except for Tina, who is taking it all in with a look of amusement on her face. Joey wants to growl at them to tell them to put their phones away, but he knows it's hopeless, so he thinks maybe this time it's OK to act the clown. So he just turns and makes a stupid pose and they snap more photos and then he changes position, and they continue to snap and laugh as they do so.

But then he remembers the newspaper cutting in Sharon's room, and the smile is gone from his face. Would she want anything to do with him if she knew he'd caused the death of that man? He doesn't even know the man's name. He doesn't want to know it, but he can picture him with his Elvis head on him. And what would Isabel think if she found out he was involved in the man's death?

'Hey, no more, please. If you don't mind,' he says like he's exhausted. And with that he grabs Sharon by the hand and heads for the bedroom, steering her in front of him round the armchairs.

13

It's like he's in his own picture book. It's called Where's Da?

He's searching on every page for him. Is he in the bedroom? He goes in there. He sees someone in the bed with his ma. He's hiding behind the newspaper. He's reading it. His da loves reading in bed. He lifts up the flap of paper so he can see. But it's not his da. It's Vinnie. He has a tiny bit of a pencil in his hand that's tied with string to his finger.

'Where's Da?' he asks. He doesn't hear an answer because now he's on the next page. He's in the kitchen. The fridge door is open. He can see the bottom half of his da. His da is a fridge door with legs. His da is wearing his Christmas pyjamas. He has two penguins on his feet. He's getting milk for his tea. His da loves milk. He calls out and his da lifts his head from behind the door. But it's not his da. It's Vinnie. He has a can of beer in his hand. 'Howya, bud!' Vinnie says. Joey isn't sure if he's talking to the can or to him. 'Where's Da?' he asks.

He's on the next page already. He's the best reader in the class. 'Where's Da?' he asks again. Now he's standing in the bathroom doorway.

He's found Da. He's in the bath. There are bubbles bouncing on the hot, foamy water. Da is a gas man. He's making a big cloud of steam. His head is up in the clouds. Joey laughs. He steps into the bathroom and he chops at the steamy wisps like he's a superhero. They swoosh off like frightened ghosts and now he can see better. But it's not steam and it makes him cough. It's not his da either. It's Vinnie. He's sitting in the water with his big hairy chest and he's got a fag stuck like a dart in his mouth.

'Where's Da?' he asks once more. But Joey can't hear what Vinnie says because he's turned over to the next page. Now he's outside and he can spot the car Da likes to drive. It's a red car. He goes over to see if his da is behind the wheel. But he's not. Then he sees the pair of long legs and the blue jeans sticking out from underneath the car. It's not his da. He's not even going to ask.

'Where's Da?' he hears someone call and when he looks, he sees the girl called Amber and she's staring at him like he's supposed to know.

'I don't know where he is! I don't know.'

'Joey!'

Sharon calls his name and kisses him awake and laughs. 'Joey!'

'What?' he says, rubbing at his lips. He opens his eyes and is so relieved it's her and not the Amber girl.

'Were you looking for your da again?'

Joey can't answer.

'Joey?'

'No! I wasn't looking for anyone. It was … It was stupid. I was in school … I think that's where I was. The teacher was asking me stuff and I kept saying I didn't know.'

She kisses him again and rubs his cheek gently with the backs of her fingers.

'Poor Joey. You really need to go and do some classes and try to get rid of all those shitty school memories.'

'I told you I will.'

He's wide awake now and reaches for his phone.

'You have plenty of time,' she says.

'I'm on an early shift today.' He stares at the phone and sees he's going to be late, but maybe not if he gets a move on.

He sits on the side of the bed and rubs sleep from his eyes.

'Joey?'

'What?'

'I didn't say anything last night, did I?'

'Say … like, what?'

'Anything stupid.'

'What? Like in front of your one, Bernice?'

'She's a bitch isn't she?'

'I don't know her well enough –'

'She is. She's a bitch. And her eyes aren't even her own.'

'What? Whose eyes has she?'

'Don't be stupid, Joey. She wears coloured contact lenses. Rodney told me.'

'People do that?'

'Oh for God's sake, Joey. She's just so false and it's really hard pretending to like her.'

'You're a very good actor,' Joey says, getting unsteadily to his feet. 'And maybe her eyes turned green when they saw you.' She laughs out loud and pulls him back down by a tug on his T-shirt. He turns and frowns at her. He hasn't time for this stuff now.

'Thank you,' she says to him and he keeps the frown going.

'Thanks for what?'

'For saying that … and for liking Rodney and Miles. I thought you'd hate them.'

'Who said I like them?'

She laughs and tugs harder on his T-shirt, like maybe she wants him back beside her. But he takes her hand gently and she releases the grip she has on him.

'I'd love to stay chatting to you all morning, Sharon, but I have to go.' He dips his head and kisses her, then heads for the shower.

14

Joey's on the street when he gets the call from Sharon. She wants to tell him that her laptop was handed in to the college and she's thrilled because everything she saved is still on it and she can get on with her work.

'And don't forget this evening.'

'What about this evening?' Joey is tired. He's done a long shift and the lad on the scooter has freaked him out and so has Weso with his talk of Vinnie and a stolen car and laptop that Quinlan wants back. All he wants to do now is get something to eat and maybe crash out in front of the telly. He'll even watch whatever shite Jackie wants to watch.

'Don't tell me you've forgotten?'

Joey stops walking and tries to think. Is it her birth-day? It can't be that. That was, like, six months ago.

'You're doing that fashion show tonight for Bernice.'

'You're kidding me!'

'You promised Bernice you'd do it.'

'I was just messing with you, Sharon. I thought it was something she was saying for a laugh.'

'I promised her you'd do it.'

'I can't be seen dead in that coat. It's like something they couldn't even give away to a charity shop.' He starts walking again and dodges pedestrians as he talks.

'You have to do it, Joey. For me. I told her you'd do it and you saw yourself how everyone just loved you in it. Plus, you'll get a chance to wear a few more of her outfits.'

'What are you talking about?'

'Bernice has a few other things she wants you to show.'

'Like what?'

'I've just seen one or two of them. One's a pair of faux leather jeans.'

'What the fuck is foh leather?'

Sharon can't help but laugh. 'Faux is French, and it's spelled F-A-U-X, Joey, just so you know. Or you can make a faux pas, which you're already an expert at.'

'Yeah, well excuse my French, Sharon, but what the fuck is faux leather about?'

'Faux leather is fake leather, Joey. Bernice wouldn't dream of using real leather in any of her creations. She's a vegan.'

'I don't give a shite what she eats. I'm not wearing a fucking leather pair of jeans.'

Sharon laughs even louder. 'Oh, come on, Joey. They're like what a biker would wear. You'll be so cool in them. And anyways it's not like anyone is going to see you.'

'You'll see me. I'll see myself.'

'Don't be ridiculous. Come on, Joey, you have to do it. You have to do it for me. Please. I promised Bernice – and if you don't do it, she's going to be really pissed with me and I can't let that happen.'

He's afraid she's going to cry and he knows now she's not as confident with her new mates as she's been letting on. He thinks of the boy on the scooter and everything Weso told him, and he still has to come up with a way to get Quinlan's laptop that was in his car back from Vinnie – that's if he still has it and hasn't already sold it on. That could be bullshit too. Vinnie probably still has the car stashed away somewhere. But Joey knows there could be more shit happening down the line so maybe he should please her and build up some brownie points.

'All right! I'll do it. But no photos put online or anywhere else. D'yeh hear me, Sharon? I see my mug on any screen and I'm finished with yeh.'

He doesn't mean it, of course. He knows Sharon knows this about him too.

'You are just the best boyfriend in the world. The best.'

He's outside Jackie's now, and he puts his phone away as he opens the door.

He can hear violin music like there's some class of small orchestra in the apartment. This is the music that Jackie now seems to like – or wants to like. He gets the whiff of something like aftershave, but then it's overpowered by the smell of her tomato sauce, which is welcome if the music isn't.

She's there in the kitchen plucking leaves off the basil plant she keeps on the windowsill and she smiles when she sees him. She has a glass of red wine in her hand. He returns her smile. Is this what married life could be like with Sharon? But he doubts it. Sharon isn't one to wait at home and do the cooking. He imagines that would be something he'd be doing, maybe he'd even like doing.

'We have a visitor,' she says and points her glass towards the settee.

When he turns, he expects to see the cop, but it's a man in a snazzy black suit with a serious face on him. He looks like an undertaker. He's got a glass of wine in his hand and he's keeping it away from his white shirt and black tie. He has a clean-cut shiny face and his black hair barely visible above his forehead, like it's slowly slipping out of sight.

But Joey knows who he is and looks at him longer than he should and makes up his mind not to like the guy.

'This is Martin,' Jackie says and she gives Joey a bit of a stare and makes a side movement with her eyes that has a command in it.

Joey obeys the signal and goes towards the man and offers him his hand. The handshake is limp like the old celery he finds at the bottom of Jackie's fridge. The man's eyes are grey and curious, like he's looking forward to hearing all about Joey from Joey himself. But Joey has no intention of giving him much suss and moves away from him towards the stool by the counter.

'I hope you're hungry,' Jackie says, as she pours boiling water into a pot and slowly drowns spaghetti in the bubbles.

'I'm starving,' he says, wanting to turn his back to the guy but knowing it's not part of the lessons on good manners that Jackie is trying to teach him.

Before sitting, he takes a cold bottle of beer from the fridge and he feels annoyed with her for letting this guy in when he just wants to chill.

'I hear you're working in the same business as myself,' Martin says to him.

'You on minimum wage too?'

The man laughs.

'You know quite well, Joey, that Martin manages the off-licence I work in. And this wine is gorgeous by the way, Martin.'

He raises his glass in salute, then swirls the contents and pokes his big ski-slope of a nose in to sniff before taking a tiny sip. Joey takes a long slug from his beer and releases a loud belch of appreciation. Jackie gives him one of her most serious frowns but says nothing.

'So, Joey, how do you like living with your aunt?' asks Martin. 'She give you a hard time like she gives me?'

Joey smiles at Jackie.

'No! She's ... she's cool,' he says, not just out of loyalty, but because it's the truth. She's cool and kind and for some reason seems to like having him living there with her.

'Yeah,' she says. 'We seem to get along much better than I'd have expected. I just have to teach him how to use the right knife and not slurp his tea or make rude noises, and of course that business with the toilet seat that all you men have difficulty with.'

Martin finds this funny but Joey is not in the mood to laugh.

Jackie turns away to prod the spaghetti strings apart. Joey has a quick look at the guy, trying to find some more reasons to dislike him. And they're not hard to find. He looks about ten years older than his aunt and he's definitely not someone that suits her. He's sitting stiffly in his seat like there's a land mine behind him that he might set off with his arse if he sat back and relaxed.

'I'm joining a choir,' Jackie announces.

'A choir?'

'Yeah. Martin runs a choir and he's looking for fresh voices.'

'Your aunt has a beautiful voice,' Martin chips in.

'Tell that to the crows that gather outside on the grass.'

'Cheeky fucker,' Jackie says, and all three of them laugh. She gives the spaghetti a stir, and it's then that Joey sees the large plaster on her finger and it looks like it's hiding something serious.

'You trying to open the wine with your bare hands?' he says, smiling up at her. 'What happened?'

'Ah ... just an incident with a customer. Well, hardly a customer.'

'The little shit,' Martin says. 'I only wish I'd been there.'

'If you'd been there, he probably wouldn't have done it, and that's what I hate about it.'

'What happened?'

'Oh ... just this ... kid comes into the off-licence and I didn't even see him enter or I'd have stopped him because he was definitely under the legal age for buying booze. But it was hard to know exactly what age he was because he had his hoodie up. I hate when they come in with their hoodies up, do you know that? I hope you don't do that, Joey, that hiding your head in a hoodie.'

'I hate those damn hoodies,' Martin says, like it's the devil himself that's selling them. Then he takes a sip from his glass.

'I don't wear them now,' Joey says to Jackie.

It's not that he doesn't like them but it's more to do with Sharon's efforts to smarten him up. 'You can't go round like a skanger wearing nothing but the same trackie all week, and with your hand slipped in the front of it playing with your balls.' That's what she actually said to him.

He takes another guzzle from the bottle and feels a little bit uncomfortable, like he can see the kid Jackie is talking about.

'Anyway, he's over by the wine, at the shelf where the most expensive stuff is kept, and he lifts up a bottle, and I can see two of his fingers are strapped together like he's broken them. I feel sorry for him. Now I'm going to chat to him instead of just telling him to leave. But just before I get to him, he drops the bottle on the floor and it smashes. And he jumps out of the way of the splashes and the broken glass like he was expecting it to fall. He just smiles at me. It's a cold smile. "Oops!" he says. Then he calmly walks out, bold as brass. It's like he did it deliberately just to annoy me. Or because he was bored. He just walked out the door and when I go out to the street, I can see there's another lad out there waiting for him with one of those electric scooters and he's minding a second one like it's a horse and they're straight out of some cowboy film. Then the two of them mount up and they're off along the path and gone.'

She holds the finger out for him to see. 'I cut it cleaning up after him.'

He wants to ask her questions about the boy, about what he was wearing, but he knows that would be a waste of time and anyway it might only spook her. Her story has spooked him.

'I wouldn't cry over spilled milk – but spilled wine, now that's entirely a different thing,' Martin says and smiles at his own joke even if no one else does.

Jackie fishes out a string of spaghetti and tests it with a bite.

'Jesus Jackie, you'll have it all eaten before we even sit down,' Joey says and he can hear Martin laugh even though it wasn't that funny.

She drains the spaghetti and Joey moves to the table and sits. Martin gets to his feet and lifts his car keys off the coffee table.

'Are you not staying for a bite to eat, Martin?' Jackie asks.

'No, I've too much paperwork to do. But I'll call you later.'

He goes to Jackie and he kisses her on the lips and gives her a quick hug and then he's gone.

'A choir?' Joey says, watching her make her quick blessing before picking up her fork and spoon.

'Yeah, what's wrong with that?'

'Nothing – except I'd say he won't have you singing any of the latest hits.'

'For fucksake, Joey, it's a choir. A church choir.'

'He'll have you going to Mass next.'

Jackie stops her hand mid-air and there's sauce clinging to the spaghetti that's dangling from her fork.

'What makes you think he goes to Mass?'

'His keyring. There was a little crucifix on it. I thought it was a bottle opener but I think he'd rather be drinking what the priests drink.'

'You can be a terrible smart arse, Joey.'

'Ah he's not that bad, Jackie. He has a great nose for the wine anyway.'

Jackie opens her mouth but just makes an 'O' rather than saying anything. She forks the food and then takes a sip of her wine. She takes up a paper napkin and dabs at the corners of her mouth before taking another napkin from the lollipop-stick basket that Isabel made for her.

'So, what if he does go to Mass?' she says as she places the extra napkin beside Joey's plate. 'You could do with a bit of religion yourself, you know.'

Joey laughs. 'Ah, I'm just pulling your chain, Jackie.'

'Yeah, well stop doing it because I'm not in the mood to be teased.'

'Why? What's wrong? Finger still sore, or are you annoyed Saint Martin didn't stop over for dinner and dessert?'

She doesn't answer, and he feels bad for being the smart arse she called him. She refills her glass and takes a long sip out of it. She pushes her plate away from her, though the food is only half eaten.

'This is delicious, Jackie,' he says.

'I'm not hungry any more.'

'What? Is it that little prick that came into the off-licence?'

'No! ... It's ...'

'What? Is that fella Martin annoying you because if he is I can ... I don't know ... give him a dig.'

'It's not him.'

'So, who is it?'

'It's that ... Vinnie.'

'Vinnie!' Now it's Joey who isn't interested in eating. 'What about Vinnie?'

'I think he wants to see me.'

'You mean ... you knew he was back before that detective guy was here?'

'Kind of.'

'He contacted you?'

'Sort of.'

'Kind of! Sort of! What the fuck?'

'Look! This guy came into the off-licence about three weeks ago. I was off that day. But he asked one of the lads about me – was I still working there – and for some reason the first person I thought of was Vinnie. But he said this guy had long hair and looked like a biker so I let it go. But then that cop turns up here – and now the incident with the kid and the wine. I've a bad feeling about it, like they're all connected in some way, like Vinnie is up to something and something bad is going to happen.'

'Three weeks! He's back here that long?'

'I don't know. But I'm thinking that maybe he just got tired of Donegal or wherever he's supposed to have been.

Or he might want to be here near his family. Well, near Isabel anyway.'

'His family!' Joey sniffs. 'He should have been more careful about his family the last time he was here.'

Jackie stares at him and there's a question in her eyes.

'I don't want to talk about it, Jackie, so don't ask me.'

He twists his fork into the spaghetti with the sauce clinging to it and then prods the fork against the big spoon the way Jackie taught him. He winds what he's gathered until it's secure enough to move to his mouth. He's hoping she'll forget to ask him any more about Vinnie.

'I think you need to talk about this, Joey.'

'Talk about what?

'Whatever is going on for you. I don't understand why it's so difficult for you to talk about him. Jesus, but there was a time years ago when he was all you'd talk about.'

'I don't want to talk about him, Jackie, because he reminds me too much about –'

'What?'

'What I was like then. How stupid I was.'

'You were never stupid, Joey. You just loved him too much to see his faults.'

Jackie looks off towards the window like her thoughts have taken her away somewhere. She smiles like to herself, then turns the smile towards Joey.

'I love – loved – him too. Even before your ma did.'

'No way!' Joey can't believe what he's hearing.

'I was the one who introduced the pair of them.'

'No way, Jackie!'

'She thought nobody could ever replace your da.' She gives a small laugh. 'And she wasn't impressed with Vinnie when she met him. Said he was full of himself. But as soon as *he* laid eyes on *her*, he dropped me like a hot potato and went chasing after her.'

'Chasing?'

'Well as good as, when you consider where your ma was working then.'

'In the bookies?'

'Yeah. She said she'd see him come in the door, like to back a horse. And he'd write on the slips of paper and hand them to her like he was making a series of bets. But what he'd write weren't the names of horses but bits of songs or lines of stupid poetry he'd made up, or the name of a fancy restaurant he wanted to bring her to and the time beside it like it was the starting time of a race.'

'And Ma fell for all that?'

'He wore her down. I suppose some girls love the chase – or at least the attention that comes with it.'

He thinks of Sharon and isn't sure she'd like to be getting bits of poems or lines from songs from him. Or maybe she would now she's in Trinity. The girl Tina pops into his head and he doesn't know what that's about.

'And when things got bad with your ma and she'd put him out, he'd come calling here to me. Always looking for sympathy. And fool that I was, I'd give it to him. Then your ma would be on the phone and he'd be there across from me listening to what she'd be saying about him and then he'd give his version of it.'

'He stole money off her that she had in her chest of drawers,' Joey says.

'He'd tell me he'd borrowed it and always paid back what he took.'

'Bullshit, Jackie. And when he worked for Quinlan, he could disappear for days and Ma wouldn't know where he'd been or who he'd been with. And he'd have loads of cash then and be throwing it about the place.'

Joey thinks of the dodgy boxes Vinnie says he's going to be selling and the fortune he says he's going to make.

'Anyway she got tired of the guards calling,' he continues, 'and her having to lie and say he'd been in the house all night. And then there was Isabel and all the promises he made to her that he never kept and Ma having to cover for him and make up good excuses as to why he couldn't go to her school play or be at her First Communion.'

The two of them are quiet, then. Jackie takes a sip of her wine and Joey sighs loudly like he's exhausted.

'What?'

'It's just so hard, Jackie.'

'What is?'

'It's just ... I don't know what to feel. Like I remember when Ma had Isabel and I was afraid they'd forget about me. I thought Vinnie definitely would. But it wasn't like that at all. He'd need to get out of the house because Isabel ... Well, she could go mad loud when she bawled. She had some lungs on her. And Ma never knew what'd be wrong with her. Then he'd want to escape. But he'd bring me with him – Ma probably made him – but we might go Karting or to some pub up the mountains, where he'd play pool with me, or poker with some of the local heads. And I'd drink Coke and eat crisps and watch the telly in the bar.'

'That was some way to educate a child,' Jackie says, shaking her head, like not doubting a word Joey is saying.

'And Ma wanted me to stay in school but I wanted out. And Vinnie sided with me. He said I could work with him. Like as though he had a regular job. That's what I mean about him, Jackie. I don't know what to feel. One minute I'm hating his guts. Like what the fuck. I should have stayed in school. And the next I'm nearly laughing out loud to myself over something crazy I remember him doing.'

'So what changed?' Jackie wants to know. She stares at him, daring him to tell her.

And he would like to tell her about the man lying on the ground, gasping for breath like he was a fish out of water. He'd like to tell her so he could breathe more easily himself.

'Quinlan!' he says. He can blame Quinlan and there's truth in that. 'Him working for Quinlan made me change my mind about him. Because it changed him. He started doing stuff that was –'

Jackie has her eyes still fixed on him. But there's only so much he can say about those times. 'And it was all the stuff with Ma too. The way he'd have her crying – the way he'd argue with her ... like he'd lose it and blame her for everything that was wrong with his life. And he could snap at me too if I didn't go along with his plans. He was always, *always*, looking for ways to make easy money. Like he'd borrow one of Quinlan's vans and he could have me helping deliver stuff and I wouldn't even know what it was I was delivering. And if I said I didn't want to do it he'd go on about how he'd saved me from school and say how disappointed he was in me that I couldn't man up for him. I hated that. That was like the worst cut of all – that I was a disappointment.'

He ropes more of his spaghetti and digs it into the sauce and swallows it, then takes a gulp of the beer. She thankfully moves her stare towards the kitchen window.

'I feel bad too, about …'

'About what?'

'Your ma. How I treated her – over him!'

'How?'

A tear spills out from the corner of her eye and runs down her cheek. She wipes it away from the side of her mouth with the tip of her middle finger.

He just gives her a weak smile. But Jackie is sitting like she's forgotten all about her food. Her phone buzzes from over by the sink and she gets up to fetch it. She taps a message as she returns, then leaves the phone by her plate on the table.

'When he finished with your ma he stayed here with me while he found a new place to live. I don't know why I let him. I just did. Like, what was I thinking?'

Joey stares at her. He feels his mouth hanging open and closes it. He's not sure exactly what she's saying, what she's admitting to. He doesn't want to go there.

'But I've met Martin now and I'm in a much better place. But if Vinnie comes back into my life, he's going to cause me huge upset because just like you, Joey, I don't know how I'm going to deal with him. And your ma keeps ringing me about him, wanting to know if I've heard anything, and asking about you, and telling me about Isabel doing her head in. And I don't know what to be saying to her. All I know is I have to steer clear of Vinnie and he needs to steer clear of me.'

Her phone buzzes and she gives a start before leaning away to check who's calling her. She stops the buzzing, then pokes her fingers in the sleeve of her cardigan searching for a tissue. Joey points at the other sleeve where the tissue is hiding. She fishes it out and wipes her eyes with it and then her mouth.

He doesn't like to see her upset. That's why he hasn't told her that he's already met Vinnie and how relieved he was to see him. His stepda had saved him from a really bad beating. How could he tell her that and have her worry about him every time he leaves her place?

'Your ma said he beat the daylights out of that fella McGinn from your estate. Is that true?'

'I don't know, Jackie. Loads of people could have done that. Besides, he had it coming to him. You should've heard the stuff he'd shout at Ma – the things he'd like to do to her.' He stops and glances at her. 'Oh look, Jackie, I don't want to talk about him now.'

'Will you just tell me what happened? There was obviously something major that caused him to do a runner and for you to move in here with me. If he did something really bad, Joey, I'd like to know.'

Joey sighs and rubs his fingers on one side of his face.

'Look, Jackie, he pulled me into something. I had to drive for him, and it turned out like … it … just turned out … like it wasn't a game any more … like, I realised people could get hurt.'

'Who got hurt?' Jackie presses him to know.

Now there's something in his right eye. It's just behind his eyelid and it's making his eye water.

'Who got hurt, Joey?' she asks again and she's staring straight at him with those big searching eyes of hers.

'I can't tell you that, Jackie. I will some time, but not yet.'

He's afraid to tell her in case she'll be so ashamed of him she'll throw him out on the street.

'I could have ended up in prison, Jackie. We both could – and we could have made everyone ashamed of us. I don't want to be that person any more. That's why I don't want anything to do with him ever again, even though …'

'Even though what?'

'Even though I'm thinking about him nearly all the time. Hoping he's come back because he's changed his ways.' He thinks of the dodgy box in Isabel's room. Those boxes aren't really illegal – are they? 'And I want to trust him, Jackie. I do. But I can't trust him because he could be back to make trouble for Quinlan the way those cops suggested. Or it could have nothing to do with Quinlan but to do with some scheme he's hatched up. Or maybe it's because Isabel asked him to come back.'

'So, which do you think it is?'

Joey sighs. 'I don't know, Jackie, I don't. I want to believe he's not here to cause trouble. But trouble finds him. It does! And it'll find you if you have anything to do with him.'

Jackie's phone buzzes once more. She doesn't look at it, like she definitely knows who it is.

'Martin probably wants to know if I'm going out so he can sneak back in,' Joey says and smiles.

'He doesn't sneak.'

They're silent for a spell, like they have so much more to say to each other but maybe they don't know if it's safe to do so.

'Anyway,' he says with a smile, nodding towards the phone, 'Off-Licence Martin won't want a dodgy customer like Vinnie anywhere about the place.'

He picks up the bottle of beer and drains it. He takes up a forkful of spaghetti, but it's cold now and he lets the fork fall back onto the plate.

'Whatever happened, Joey, maybe you need to make some sort of reparation for it?'

'What's that supposed to mean?'

'Reparation? It's like restorative justice, you know, where you maybe find the person that you did wrong to, and write a letter saying how sorry you feel for what happened.'

'Oh my God!'

'What?'

'You were talking to Sharon ... about that stuff?'

'Yeah. I was asking her about her course and she told me all about the project she's doing.'

'She gave me a lecture about it.'

'Oh my God, she's just buzzing, Joey. She's going to make a great social worker. And that sounds like a brilliant idea ... you know ... that reparation thing.'

'Well, I think it is about more than writing a letter, Jackie.'

'You could do your own version of it, Joey.'

'What?' he says. 'Write a letter and they show it to the cops?'

'You don't sign it, you eejit. You just say how sorry you are.'

'I'm not going to do that, Jackie. No way.'

'Well then, go into a church and light a candle and ask for forgiveness. It's not as good, but at least it's something.'

Joey laughs out loud. 'What? Like going to confession?'

'You don't have to go near a priest, Joey. But sometimes it's good to go into a church and sit and light a candle and be humble enough to ask for forgiveness.'

'Ah for God's sake, Jackie. You and your religion crap.'

'It's not crap. It's what I believe in. And I'm telling you now, Joey, you won't feel good about yourself ever again unless you do something to make up for what you did wrong.'

His phone pings and he knows it's Sharon, wondering if he's ready. He glances at the screen.

'Sharon?' Jackie asks.

'Yeah.'

'Are you going out?'

'Yeah. I have to help her with something.'

'With what?'

'I just have to help out with a stupid fashion show one of her arty friends is putting on.'

Jackie laughs. 'Just make sure they don't have you on the catwalk.'

'No way that's going to happen,' he says, getting to his feet.

He knows it *is* going to happen. But he'll do it to make Sharon happy. He stands up suddenly and takes his plate to the sink.

'Leave everything. I'll tidy up.'

'Are you sure?' he says.

'Yeah, I have my own penance to do.'

He uses the spoon to eat what's left of his dinner. He stuffs it into his mouth because he's not sure what kind of arty farty food they'll have at this fashion gig. That's if they have any at all, because from what Sharon says about them, they just seem to live on popcorn.

'And Joey,' Jackie calls to him as he's standing there checking his phone for more messages.

'What?'

'Just so you know. It was my idea you come live here. It wasn't your ma's. And I wasn't sure it would work out. But it has. I love you ... being here. OK?'

'And I like it here too, Jackie.'

'And you're not a disappointment to me, Joey. Remember that!'

'For fucksake, Jackie,' he says, and he's out the door before he starts bawling like a kid in front of her.

15

They're somewhere off Thomas Street. They're in a room at the back of a sorry-looking old building that's in the process of becoming some grungy sort of art space. All the walls have been painted white and the pipes and cable ducts in the high ceiling have been exposed, like maybe they could be part of some exhibition. More likely there's not enough money to cover them. It used to be a gym, Rodney told him, and they're going to call it an art gym when it's ready to open. Joey sniffs at the idea and thinks it won't be open any time soon, but Rodney says art spaces don't need any furniture, just decent walls and a toilet.

Miles and Rodney were here when he arrived, but they've disappeared outside. He imagines they've gone to the pub for a sneaky pint, or they're smoking a joint in the laneway beside the building. He wishes he was with them.

Someone had the good sense to set up a table with wine and beer just inside the main entrance. But all the beer bottles had weird labels on them. He grabbed a Five Lamps one that Miles introduced him to. Jackie has been bringing home the odd bottle of this craft stuff and talking about it like it's wine. He's killed telling her that it's the price that matters for him and not the taste, once it's not piss.

He's wearing his favourite black T-shirt, his straight leg jeans, his black soft leather runners and the faded denim jacket that Sharon said she likes. He's gulping down the beer now as he waits for Sharon to gather together the clothes he's to change into. The room they're in is some sort of makeshift dressing room at the back of the building. It looks like someone knocked the walls between two changing rooms, but kept all the lockers and the painted signs on the walls that point towards the toilets and the shower area.

The room has about ten of those clothes rails with little wheels on them and there's an assortment of outfits crowding for space on each of them. There are art heads beside each one and all of them jabbering and poking at clothes like they can't decide what to wear. And there's a few he sees who are already trying on outfits, with other heads in close attendance poking at them and pulling at sleeves, or sticking pins in hems, or adjusting collars, or just plain 'foostering', as his ma might say.

There are four girls in a cluster beside this one rail and one of them is wearing this black pin-stripe suit, but with running shorts instead of trousers. Where the fuck is she working? The other three are wearing what look like different bits of her missing outfit, like they're jigsaw pieces and she's to be the finished picture. Maybe they've all been smoking weed or maybe he's just dreaming this shit.

He waves at Bernice when he thinks she's spotted him, but she hasn't. She's with a skinny girl who's wearing something like it's made from a shower curtain and Bernice is trying to get the zip to open or close – he's not sure which.

There are young arty-looking people all about the place. There's a guy with a head of curly hair that must be a wig and he's pulling at clothes on the rails like he's looking for something in particular. Poor fucker, Joey thinks. He obviously can't find what he's looking for because his hands disappear into his hair in exasperation and then he's off to annoy Bernice, who points off to the back of the room where Sharon is loading clothes onto one of her arms.

And as Sharon walks towards him, he sees her stop to talk to a girl on her knees in front of a young couple who could be going to an Addams Family wedding. Now why couldn't he have been asked to wear one of their outfits? But of course Bernice is into a totally different look. She has this outfit on; it's a cardigan made for a giant that looks like it's been put together from four different coloured sheep. It's looping down all over the place and she has to keep pulling her sleeves up to her elbow so she can work with the shower curtain girl. And the place is cold and he thinks all these models will have their arses frozen off them before the evening is out.

He wonders what he's let himself in for but it's too late to pull out now.

'Did you not read the sign?' Sharon snaps at him the second she's back with her collection.

'What sign?'

'Oh, never mind! Just drink it back quick before Bernice sees you.'

He puts the bottle down on the fold-up table that's beside him. It's one of those rickety tables you use for wallpapering your gaff. He nearly made the mistake of sitting on it when he came in, not realising what it was, with the assortment of clothes that had been placed there.

'Don't leave it there,' Sharon warns and grabs the bottle and stashes it on a shelf beside a row of white candles that throw flickering little shapes onto the wall behind. He knows her nerves are frazzled.

'What the fuck is this place?' he asks, though he knows already.

'It used to be a gym but it went bust. The landlord is Bernice's uncle, by the way, so I don't want you doing anything to piss her off. Do you hear me, Joey?'

She plonks her clothes heap onto the wallpaper table and it bends like a hammock from the weight. She separates the clothes while Joey's attention is taken up by the sight of Tina, who has been in the room all along but he hasn't noticed her until now. Or maybe he didn't recognise her because her jet-black hair is down and tied in a loose ponytail that hangs from one of her shoulders. Her lips are glossed with dark red lipstick. But it's her T-shirt his eyes are drawn to. They've got Scrabble letters printed on the front saying shirt but the 'R' has fallen out. She notices his gaze and waves at him and he waves back at her and gives her a thumbs up. Sharon notices where his attention has gone.

'Tina and Bernice don't really get on so don't say too much nice stuff about her T-shirts.'

'OK,' he says.

He can't help himself but laugh when the girl deliberately turns away from him so he can see what's written on the back of her T-shirt. She's got the letters 'C – N T' written there in Scrabble lozenges. There's two possible letters beneath to insert and they're 'A' and 'U'. She points off towards Bernice and then back to him and silently mouths one of the letters. He laughs out loud, and she laughs with him, and then she's away towards a girl who's trying on some sort of hat that might just be a cardboard flower pot.

'That Tina's always looking for notice,' Sharon says.

'I like her,' Joey says before he can stop himself.

Sharon doesn't say anything, just turns her face away. Bernice comes towards them with her green eyes in and Sharon cooks up a smile for her.

'Are you sure he wants to do this?' she says to Sharon, like she's also frazzled.

'He's been talking 'bout nothing else,' Sharon says and reverses her sharp elbow so it touches Joey's stomach.

Bernice glances at his jeans and runners. 'They have to go, you know.'

'Of course,' Sharon says. Bernice lifts what looks like a pair of leather shorts from the table and hands them to Joey.

'What?' Joey says, gaping at them. He glances at Sharon but she's not returning his gaze. He can feel the elbow press against his stomach.

'He's to wear these! And give him the white T-shirt with the red stains I showed you for under the coat. And

I'll get you the Docs.' She walks off to the other side of the room, where there's another table with shoes on it.

'What the fuck, Sharon. You said leather jeans like a biker might wear. What's this for? A fucking girls' tricycle?'

'You promised me Joey! So you'd better do whatever she asks you to do.'

Then Bernice is back before he can make any sort of protest and she hands him what look like ski boots or maybe they're those hospital boots they give you when you fracture your leg – except these have laces as well as a multitude of zips. He stares at Sharon, then nods at the boots. How the fuck is he supposed to get himself into those?

'They zip up from the back.'

He checks where she's pointing and he can see the long zip track she means. 'You'll be just fantastic, Joey,' Bernice is saying. 'In fact you're so fantastic you're going to be on twice.'

'Twice!' The word comes out like a whisper.

'Yeah, the first time you go out you'll be wearing the coat, shorts, vest and boots – and this glove.' Joey stares at her hand and sees the creased red glove she holds. Bernice is still talking and he realises he'd better listen. He takes the glove off her and tries it on.

'I like the way you've gelled his hair, Sharon,' she says.

'Thanks!' Sharon answers.

Joey finds a smile he's surprised he could muster. He wouldn't let Sharon touch his hair. And at least they're not asking him to wear some sort of hat.

'Sharon showed you how I want you to walk?' Bernice says. She eyes Sharon and Joey sees her face colour a little.

'Joey won't let you down,' Sharon says.

Bernice frowns at Joey and he nods. 'Yeah, yeah, I've seen this shit before,' he says.

Sharon leans in and pinches him on the elbow.

'Not the clothes,' Joey blurts out, 'the way of walking. I've seen it before and anyway she showed me how to do it.'

Then Bernice is gone off to help the Addams Family and open or close the shower curtain girl. Sharon then tells him it's time for him to change and he stares at the faux leather shorts and shakes his head at all the gear gathered on the table.

'You fuckin' owe me big time, Sharon,' he says. She lifts out the coat and the T-shirt.

'Well, at least the T-shirt is like something you'd wear,' she says and manages a faux smile. She takes up the gear and nods towards a small curtained area in the corner of the room. 'Change in there! Just make sure all the girls are out of it first, though.'

Joey stares where she's nodding. 'And when you come back in from showing the first outfits, I'll have the rest of them waiting for you.'

'What are they?'

'They're more to your liking I'd say. There's a pair of her jeans –'

'Her jeans?'

'Not *her* jeans! They're jeans she's designed. And there's a pair of black brogue shoes and a torn tie dye T-shirt that's done to look like dried-in oil stains.'

Joey does a quick scan and sees the items.

'For fucksake,' he says when he sees the jeans have zips at both knees but there's half a leg missing.

'Don't even ask,' Sharon says, like all of a sudden she doesn't want to be here any more than he does.

He pulls on the shorts and can't believe they fit him. Sharon pokes her head in through the curtains and he can see the smile she's trying to conceal. He says nothing to her because now it's all too late. He tries on the boots. He wants to wear them without socks, but Sharon won't hear of it. Her head disappears, then returns almost immediately and she hands him some sort of tiny nylon sock yoke to stop him from getting athlete's foot.

'Like an athlete would wear this shite,' he mutters down to the floor. He just wants to run from the place.

Once he emerges from the changing room he can hear the hubbub of voices coming from out the front and the chairs scraping the floor. There was no one there on the way in – it was just three lines of chairs on either side of a long strip of white carpet. The carpet led to a small circular platform covered in red, and then the white strip continued down the other side and dead-ended at a black painted wall that had a skull shape stencilled on it.

'Look, it's for charity,' Sharon says. She knows he's ready to bolt. 'And if you make a run for it now, I'll never speak to you again – ever!'

'All right!' he snaps, 'but there'd better be no one out there that knows me.' He remembers he still has the pair of shades. He had them in his jacket pocket and he's transferred them to the coat. He dips his hand in but he's not sure how many pockets are in the fuckin' thing or where his glasses have disappeared to. 'It's a clown's fuckin' coat,' he says in exasperation.

'Shut up saying that,' Sharon snaps at him, and Bernice is at the curtain like they're backstage in some theatre and she's beckoning to them because it's his turn to make an entrance.

He finds the shades and places them firmly on his nose as he heads towards her. But Bernice snatches the shades off his head just before he steps through and now all he can see in front of him is bright white light splashed on the floor. And like for the first time he realises there's been music playing and it's like something out of *Mad Max*.

Is he supposed to be some sort of lunatic driver out to do damage, or is he one of the good guys that's going to save the planet? He reckons Bernice has him down as the first kinda fucker. Someone is going wild with a smoke machine and puffing out chunks of the white stuff and there's wisps of it clinging to him already and there's a layer like low cloud covering the bottom of the white track, but thank fuck, he can see the way he has to go. It's about all he can see. But he'll keep his eyes on the twisting carpet and then it's up one side of the platform and down the other side as far as the skull and then he'll turn and retrace his steps.

He can about make out the tips of the audience's feet poking out into the smoke and he hopes there's no lanky fuckers present. Is this what it's like to be an actor on stage? He is an actor. Yeah, that's what he is. He's an actor who doesn't have to speak a line, just walk one instead.

He gets a shock at the amount of feet and hopes they keep them to themselves. 'Walk in rhythm to the music,' Sharon had said, 'and keep your eyes raised and your face expressionless.' He'll have no trouble doing either.

When he gets to the platform, he's been told to remove the coat and hang it from one shoulder and then step down the other side and walk like he owns the world.

'Please don't fuck it up, Joey.' He hears Sharon's voice in his ear. He pictures the anxiety written all over her face, like she's going to be exposed. He'll get through this for her sake.

The music is punkish loud and he thinks of Weso and the crazy look he could get in his eyes when he was high on his cocktail of beer and pills. He knows he often wore that same glassy look himself. Now he can use this memory to help him. He'll strut like they did after they walked unscathed from all those cars they raced the shit out of. Yeah, he's with Weso! He can do this. He can do it if he keeps his eyes forward and pretends Weso is strutting beside him and they've just spent the last couple of hours zig-zagging on the motorway or making doughnuts on the backroads that lead out of the estate and up into the hills.

He has the strut going and he's keeping time with the music that's driving him forward. There's someone scream-singing, sounding demented, and there's a lunatic loose at the drums, and then it's a chorus of wild voices, screeching like everyone should flee from him, and he's pounding along like this soundtrack is the soundtrack of his former life and now he just needs to keep it going, keep it going, keep it going to the wall-skull and back. Yeah, he can do it one more time for Sharon. He's reached the platform. It's like an altar, he thinks. It is an altar and he's the mad high priest, or maybe the devil himself, and he hopes everyone in the audience has a long spoon in their pockets. All he has to do is stand on the platform and remove the coat. That's what he does. He slips it off and lets it dangle from one shoulder. There's a new sound and he realises it's applause. They're clapping him, and whistling and cheering like they really like how he can strut his stuff. He kinda likes it too, gets a sudden buzz from the adulation, from the way he's transforming these bits of gear into something manly and futuristic.

The applause dies down and he's off again and he hears the engine of a formula one racing car and he knows he's meant to be driving this forward now. He's behind the wheel in the cramped space, but the road in front is wide and free and he presses his foot down so he can accelerate home.

But there's another sound from somewhere near him. It's laughter. It's some fucker laughing his head off, laughing like maybe he's a lunatic in the car with him. It's not Weso's laugh. Where is Weso now? He's on his own. He stops. He wants to see who the fuck is making the sound. He knows he shouldn't stop, shouldn't stare into the crowd. But there's a fucker out there who's taking the piss. He hears the sound again and he can't help but make two fists, but that makes the laughter grow louder and now it sounds like there could be a few more joining in. Are they laughing at the guy because of his crazy laugh or are they laughing at him? Then there's voices asking for hush and he moves on again and hurries now like he's frightened and being chased rather than strutting away from some scene of carnage he's just caused.

Sharon is at the curtain as he comes through and he barges past her, whipping off the glove and flinging it on the floor.

'I'm not doing any more of this shit,' he snarls at her and doesn't wait for her response. He takes up his own clothes and heads for the curtained area, where he can get back to himself.

'You have to go on again, Joey,' he hears her say from outside, but he's too annoyed to even answer her. 'Please, Joey! Just one more time. Do it for me. Please!'

'No way, Sharon! No way I'm going out there to be laughed at.'

Then he's walking past her and stops when he realises that he has to go out through the curtain in order to exit. No fucking way he's going to walk once more on that runway.

'That's it, Sharon. No way I'm going out there again and I don't give a shite what Bernice says to you.'

He has done enough for her. She sighs and looks like she might suddenly cry, but he doesn't care if her face floods with tears.

'I have to get out of here,' he gasps, like he suddenly needs air.

He stands, not knowing what direction to take. If he has to, he'll hide in the curtained area until the whole fuckin' show is finished.

'There's a door over there to the alleyway,' Sharon says pointing towards the toilet signs and he sees the door she means.

He can't even look at her as he heads for the exit, not caring what she or anyone else thinks about his desertion.

He's out in the alleyway and is heading for the street when he sees a guy having a smoke and something seems to be amusing him like he's remembering a great joke he's recently heard.

The guy turns as Joey goes to walk past him. He stares into Joey's face, then points all his fingers at Joey like he needs him to stay clear or he'll only start his laughing once more.

'Do you want a fuckin' dig?' Joey cries out, stopping in front of the guy and making a fist that he'll let him have if he doesn't get rid of the grin. And then he recognises the guy.

'Magpie! What the fuck?'

Magpie Dolan goes to draw on the smoke but can't because he's grinning so hard.

'For fucksake, it wasn't that funny.'

Magpie obviously thinks it was that funny, because it takes him a few more seconds to calm himself enough to take a drag from his smoke.

'Ah Jaysus, Joey. I thought I was going to piss myself. And I'd have paid double the entrance money if I'd known you were going to be there.'

'OK, but you can cut it out now.'

'Sorry, Joey! But the music was so loud I didn't think anyone would hear me.'

'Well, they did.'

'Yeah, obviously, cos they fucked me out. And I didn't get my money's worth. Hey wait! I did get my money's worth.'

'Just shut up about it, OK?'

Magpie is quiet and takes a drag from his cigarette and then he takes the box of smokes out of his jacket and offers it to Joey.

'I don't smoke any more,' he says, then changes his mind. 'Ah fuck it. I'll take one.'

He takes a cigarette out of the box and Magpie lights it for him.

Joey draws on it and lets the smoke go way down his throat. He coughs and Magpie Dolan laughs.

'You're losing your cool, Joey.'

'Yeah, and don't I know it. Fucking Sharon and her arty farty Trinity pals.'

'I promise I won't spill a word of this to anyone. Though, like, every second person in there had their phones out.'

Joey doesn't want to think about it. He's just wondering how it's Magpie Dolan that's in front of him. It's the hair that's different from that time he saw him in Richie's shop. It's like someone took him aside and had a word in his ear about appearances being important.

'What did you do to your hair?'

'It's called the Caesar cut. Sharon got me to get it.'

'You're pally with Sharon?'

'Yeah. Bumped into her on the first day. Now she's like ... helping me fit in. She said the new cut gives me a classy look, makes me look interesting – but you know how Caesar ended up.'

'Yeah,' Joey says, though he hasn't a clue what happened to the guy, except maybe way back he had something to do with raising a couple of wolves in Rome. Maybe they ate him or something.

But he hasn't seen much of Magpie since those early years in secondary school. He was the only one in the class he really liked, but Weso gave him a hard time and gave him the name 'Magpie' when he wore a Newcastle United jersey to school as part of No Uniform Day.

'I haven't really seen you or spoken to you since that time of the –'

'Yeah,' Magpie says like he remembers those days exactly. 'And I shouldn't even be talking to you. You were such a prick then. You and that fucker Weso. Still can't believe he's Sharon's brother. But you did me a favour the pair of you.'

'Yeah?'

'Yeah, I just got out of there and changed schools. Though it took me half an hour longer in the morning to get there. So you owe me all that time I lost, Joey.'

'You left?'

'You mean you never noticed?'

'Fuck it, Magpie, I was never really there.' Joey holds the fag between his fingers and stares at the guy. 'You left because of us? Because of me and Weso?'

'Yeah. Why are you surprised? There's guys I know who didn't go to that school at all once they knew the pair of you were going there.'

'Jesus, Magpie. I didn't know that.'

'Well, now you do.'

'But how did you end up here, at this gig?'

'Sharon invited me.'

'Can't believe ye met up on the first day.'

'Yeah, and I bumped into her again when registering for the Trinity rowing club.'

'Rowing? You and Sharon? Rowing?'

'Yeah. It's deadly. Sharon hasn't come along yet, but I've done a couple of sessions. Down the Liffey first thing on a Sunday morning. It's massive.'

Joey stares at Magpie like he's seeing him for the first time. He didn't notice it in Richie's shop because of what was happening outside, but he can see now how Magpie has changed. He's tall now, taller than Joey, and he must be in the gym a lot from the way he's filling the black T-shirt he's wearing.

'Can't believe you're in Trinity as well. How the fuck did they let you in there?'

'I got good Leaving Cert results. I'm doing computer science. And I've a job in a bar in town as well as the grant, so –'

'Computer science? I don't even know what that's about, Magpie.'

'That's another thing!'

'What?'

'Nobody knows me as Magpie there. And I don't want to be called that name any more.'

Joey looks him up and down. 'Yeah, OK!'

'You were the one who gave me the name.'

'Me? I thought it was –'

'It was you, Joey.'

'OK! Sorry 'bout that.'

They both draw smoke from their cigarettes down into their chests, then blow it off to the side. Then Magpie flicks the butt away and watches it spark off the cobbled laneway.

'I should make tracks,' he says. He glances up to the top of the alleyway like there's someone waiting for him.

'You meeting someone?'

'No. Just thinking about walking home.'

'Walking?'

'Yeah, I'm living in town now. I hear you're in with your Aunt Jackie.'

'Yeah.'

'So you're not hanging with Vinnie any more?'

'How do you know about Vinnie?'

'For fucksake, Joey, the whole world knows about Vinnie. And everyone was glad to see the back of him, wherever it was he fled to.'

Joey takes another pull on the cigarette and this time when he lets the smoke down into his chest, he feels a lot better, like it's filling a hole that needs filling. Vinnie! He'd forgotten all about him. But he's not going to start thinking about him now and have the night ruined even further.

'I deserved that,' Joey says.

'What?'

'You laughing at me like that. I was an awful prick those years.'

'You were a bollix. I don't even know why I was desperate back then that you'd like me.'

'I did like you.'

'Yeah but ...'

'Weso!'

'Yeah.'

'Dickhead!'

'Yeah.'

Then he's off laughing once more like he's thought of something else.

'What?' Joey says.

'The state of yeh! I had to take time off work tonight just to come to this thing and I was fuckin' raging. But now – hey, it was worth it just to see you strutting along there in your leather shorts. I had a pain in me chest from laughing. Thought I was going to get a heart attack.'

'Fucking Sharon and her new friends. And they weren't leather. They were faux.'

'Ah yeah, that makes them OK, I suppose,' Magpie says with a grin. Then he's guffawing again and coughing like there's still some smoke left in his chest.

'You tell anyone about what you saw and I'll have to let all Sharon's friends know about your nickname.'

He turns to go but then stops. 'You don't even remember my real name, do yeh?'

Joey has to think. 'Of course I do. It's Steo.'

'Stephen.'

'Well excuse me.'

He readies himself once more to go. 'Hey, hang on there, Stephen.'

'What?'

'I'm fuckin' gaspin' for a pint.'

16

He texts Sharon to let her know he's found the fucker who was laughing at him. She texts back with a worried emoji, and begging him not to do anything stupid. She's in enough shit with Bernice and doesn't want more upset. He sends her a selfie of himself and Stephen and tells her the name of the bar they've chosen for a quiet pint.

And it is quiet. It's an old man's pub with a long wooden bar on one side with a couple of old-timers pulled in against it and studying their pints like they're art exhibits.

There are wide wooden floorboards going the length of the room and behind the bar is a forest of framed mirrors and spirit bottles and dark wooden cubby holes holding old books and an assortment of copper jugs. The wall opposite has a display of old black and white photographs of Dublin streets with a long shelf beneath and bar stools that are all empty. The only other furniture in the room is some rectangular wooden tables and little faux-leather-topped stools gathered round them.

Faux leather! He'll be spotting the stuff everywhere from now on.

He's delighted to be in such a quiet hideaway, even though there's a group of middle-aged women down near the back and one of them has a machine gun laugh he knows will annoy him. Stephen brings him a pint of lager and he doesn't care what fucker brewed it.

'Hope that's not faux lager,' Stephen says and laughs.

'What the fuck was I thinking?'

'Sharon's idea, yeah?'

'No, it was that Bernice one with her notions.'

'She's gorgeous, though.'

'Yeah,' Joey says. He's had enough of her, but he has to admit she's more than nice-looking.

'She's outa my league, though,' Stephen says.

'Maybe not any more with your Caesar head on yeh and the muscles you're getting from pulling like a dog in that row boat.'

Stephen glances at him and smiles; then he sniffs like he knows it's not ever going to come true.

They're quiet then. Joey isn't sure how to talk to the guy. All he can remember is teasing him and treating him like shit. Maybe if he'd hung around with him instead of Weso, he'd be in Trinity as well. But meeting him again is giving him a chance to be, like, friendly towards him – maybe even have him as a buddy. Sharon would be pleased at least. He takes a long sip from the pint and tries to think of something to say.

He's chatted to Miles and Rodney and enjoyed listening to them argue over the merits of a particular painting, or debate some article they've both read online. Joey hasn't read anything in over a year, other than texts and other amusing crap on his phone.

He hasn't been out socialising with anyone else other than Sharon in a year, and before that there was just a mess of drink and drugs and he can't remember any one decent conversation he had with anyone. Sharon and Jackie are the only two people he feels comfortable talking to. He can't spend long visiting his ma and Isabel because there's too much of his shitty past out there. Now he looks at Stephen checking his phone and wonders if he's bored. He's not sure what he should say to him. He knows he should apologise for all the crap he put him through.

They're perched on two high stools with Joey facing the bar and Stephen beside him. The door opens and a young guy who must be only Isabel's age enters and glances towards them, before walking past. The barman gives him a frown and the boy points to the toilet and the barman nods and loses interest. The boy looks like one of those scooter lads except he hasn't bothered to hide his head in his hoodie. But he has the rest of the gear. Joey keeps his eye on the toilet door and the boy is out again like he's changed his mind about taking a piss or else he didn't like the look of the place. He glances towards Joey as he leaves but doesn't catch his eye. Stephen turns to see what Joey is looking at.

'What's going on?'

'Nothing!' He drinks deep from his pint.

'But I was an eejit,' Stephen is saying, but Joey has zoned out and is still thinking about the boy and what he might have been up to. 'You're not doing that any more, are yeh?'

'What?' Joey says, coming back into the room.

'Robbing cars.'

'You think Sharon would want anything to do with me if I was? That was the first thing she said to me when I told her I fancied her – well, that and the fact that Weso might cave my head in if he thought I was with her.'

'You know he's working for that tosser Quinlan now?'

'Yeah,' Joey says.

'Sharon has disowned him, and she'll disown you too if you have anything to do with him or Quinlan.'

Joey doesn't want to talk about Weso or Quinlan or even about Sharon. His head needs a break from it all. So he switches the conversation to working in the shop and the head-the-balls he gets to meet there. Stephen tells him about trying to fit into Trinity and his part-time job in the bar he's working in, and moving out of his gran's gaff to stay in a crappy house with three lads from the midlands.

They've switched to cider and they're on their third pint when Sharon comes in the door and glances about the bar like she's not impressed.

Stephen climbs quickly to his feet and gives her a hug and then he's off to the loo, so Sharon can give Joey his telling-off without an audience.

'You want a drink?' Joey asks her.

She glances at the bar like there's nothing there she could ever let touch her lips.

'I'm not staying.'

'Come on, Sharon. How could I go on again after that?'

'It was just Stephen. Nobody else was laughing at you.'

'I heard more than Stephen.'

'All right, Joey, I'm sure there were a few laughing at him, but nobody could hear much anyway with the music.'

'Anyway, how did it go?'

Sharon makes a long sigh from right down in her chest. He wishes she would sit down. He pulls one of the bar stools closer to her but she ignores the signal.

'It was OK. Bernice wasn't happy.'

'About what?'

'What the fuck do you think, Joey? She wasn't happy about you. And then she had nobody to wear the rest of the gear.'

'What? It wouldn't fit anyone.'

'No! So I had to go out.'

Joey starts to laugh even though he knows he shouldn't, but the thought of Sharon in the one-legged jeans is funny.

'You had to do the walk?'

'Yeah.'

'I'm sorry I didn't see that. But I'd say you were better at it than I was.'

'Bernice got crabbed even more because of Tina and her T-shirts. Everyone loved them and wanted to know where they could buy them.'

'Hey, I'm not surprised. Those T-shirts are gorgeous.'

'Gorgeous?'

'For fucksake, Sharon!' He's just about to try and defend himself, but he stops because Stephen is back from the toilet. Sharon moves out of his way to let him sit back on his seat.

'Are yeh not staying for a drink, Sharon?'

'I'm joining Bernice and the gang over in Arthur's.'

'You want us to join you?' Joey asks, already knowing her answer.

'No. And you get that smile off your face, Stephen. It was all your fault in the first place.'

'You should've warned me, Sharon. You shoulda!'

Joey has enough drink taken to allow him to smile, but it doesn't seem to impress Sharon. She blows air from her mouth upwards to dislodge her fringe, which is sticking to her eyebrows. Now her gaze is meant only for Joey.

'And I don't know if it's a good idea to come round to my place tonight either,' she says. 'Bernice is going to be there with her mates and I don't think she'll want to see you.'

'OK,' Joey says.

There's no way he's going to obey that order. Jackie is having Martin over and he's picked up the vibe that he should make himself scarce for the night.

It's nearly midnight when Joey and Stephen stagger their way onto the street where Sharon's apartment is. There's a squad car just up from the door with the blue light flashing. There's nobody in it or near it. But Miles is there on the steps smoking a cigarette like he's minding the car for the coppers.

Sharon! Has something happened to her? Joey leaves the doddering Stephen in his wake and runs along the footpath, suddenly sober.

'What's going on, Miles?' he says dreading to hear that Sharon is in trouble. 'Is Sharon OK?'

'It's not Sharon. It's Rodney.'

'What's happened to Rodney?'

Stephen is out of breath behind him and leaning against the railing like it's holding him up. But Joey needs to go in and find out what's happened. He wants to hear it from Sharon herself, but Miles holds him by the sleeve.

'I don't think you should go in there, Joey,' he says.

'Why not?'

'Because of what happened.'

'What? I just got pissed off because that eejit there behind me was laughing at me.' He points with his thumb to Stephen, who now has his arse hovering over the step like he's attempting to make it land.

'It's not that.'

'What is it then? What happened?'

'Rodney got beaten up on the way home.'

'By who?'

'Three young fellas.'

'Because he's gay!'

'No!'

'Why, then?' He remembers the lad coming into the pub like the two incidents are connected.

'I thought you might know the answer to that.'

'What the fuck are you talking about, Miles?'

'"Tell Joey to get a move on!" That's what one of them said before they went off on their e-scooters.'

Joey can't believe what he's hearing. He goes to dart past and get inside to hear for himself what happened, but Miles holds him by the sleeve once more.

'You'll only make things worse if you go in there now.'

'Then send Sharon down to me, Miles,' he says like he's begging. And he is begging.

'She doesn't want to talk to you,' Miles says.

Joey feels the anger rise up inside him. This isn't his fault. He's just trying to mind his own business, stay away from trouble. Vinnie was supposed to sort everything out with Quinlan about the car and whatever else he took. Then Sharon is in the doorway and Miles goes away inside. Joey looks up at her and sees her eyes blazing with anger.

'I told you, Joey. I warned you. Keep your shit away from me.'

'This isn't my shit,' Joey pleads, but she's not listening.

'It is your shit. It's always your shit. Like I know it was your shit over my stolen laptop and that cop that suddenly appeared. I told you this is my time. This is my place now, my home, and I'm not going to have it fucked up on me because of whatever it is you've done.'

'I haven't done anything,' Joey protests as he climbs the steps towards her. But she puts out her hand to ward him away.

'It's Vinnie, Sharon! He's back down here and Quinlan is looking for him and he thinks I know where he is. But I don't know. I don't want to know. I don't want anything to do with him ever again.'

'Well, you'll have to find him and tell him to fuck off away from here because he's only going to bring misery like the last time. And yeah, I know it was him and my brother who were stealing all those catalytic converters off those cars. And I think you might have been part of it too, even though Wesley says you weren't. And if you were involved, Joey, you need to do something about it.' She pauses to rub the tears away from her face. 'I want to believe you've changed, Joey. I do. But I don't think that's ever going to happen if Vinnie is here. Something bad is going to happen. I know it is! And I don't want any part of it. So, me and you are finished, Joey.'

'Finished?' Joey can't believe his ears.

Stephen, the fuckin' eejit, groans and pukes over the step. Joey jumps away and Sharon steps back.

'See! He's only with you a few hours and already you have him fucked up.' She turns and disappears inside. Joey turns towards the street and there's just the empty squad car and him and Stephen.

Joey grabs Stephen by the elbow. Stephen turns up his drunken eyes and there's sadness in them.

'Finished?' he cries. 'Fucksakejoeythatsafuckin-tragicky!'

'You're the fuckin tragicky, Magpie. Now you get to your feet and tell me where you live so I can get us both a taxi.'

Magpie – Stephen – tries to do what Joey says and laughs at his own attempt to rise.

'I don't want ... to puke ... on Sharon's lovely step,' he says, managing to sit once more.

17

He's playing Scrabble with Sharon and Isabel. And Tina is there as well. She's made the word EYES and she's laughing at him because he has REPARATION crammed together on his little wooden ledge and he's asking her to help him. But Sharon is upset with him for taking too many letters out of the box lid and she's annoyed with Tina because she's not playing the game the way it's supposed to be played. He asks Isabel to help him with his letters because he doesn't want to annoy Sharon. But Isabel says it's already a word and he should look it up. And she shows him the word she's made and it's DADADADA and he says that's not a word but she says he's stupid and Sharon stands up suddenly and knocks over the board and scatters all the letters on the floor and then he hears Isabel shouting at him that he's a pig he's a pig

He shoots up in the bed like he needs air and he stares around the room, not sure where he is. He rubs at his fingers like he's taking off a glove. He's not a pig. But there's a pig in the room. He can hear a grunting sound, like the pig has made his way into his bed. But it's not his bed. His head is pounding and his mouth is paper-dry. He's on the end of someone's bed – Stephen's? – listening to someone – Stephen? – snoring from somewhere near his feet.

He lets his toes feel the floor and he sits at the side of the bed while he thinks about what he should do.

Sharon says she's finished with him. She said he needs to find Vinnie and talk to him so things can get back to how they were. He did talk to him! And Vinnie said he'd go and sort things with Quinlan. But he hasn't. But now how can he tell Vinnie any of the bad stuff that's happened because of those lads with the scooters. Vinnie will only want to go and attack Quinlan or do something stupid to one of the scooter heads, like he did to Ginsey.

But he's afraid also of what Quinlan might do next. Will he go after Sharon? Or his ma? Or maybe he might want to do something to Isabel? And how can he find out if Vinnie has a laptop belonging to Quinlan, if he doesn't visit Vinnie and ask him?

He knows he has to talk to Vinnie again to find out if he's even bothered to meet Quinlan. But first he has to do something about all the stuff that's disturbing his sleep every night; the stuff that has him waking up gasping for breath. He remembers the words from the dream. He remembers Jackie's advice. He remembers

Sharon's bedroom and the newspaper cutting left on the floor. Maybe she left it there deliberately for him to see? She said if he was involved he needs to do something about it. He was involved. He's let her down, disappointed her, brought nothing but trouble into her life. He pulls out his wallet and fishes out the piece of paper and unfolds it.

18

The sea is to one side of him and fancy houses on the other that are at the end of long gardens. He sees the school gates and the school building behind and the sign with the name written large on it. He holds the newspaper clipping out in front of him so he can examine it to be sure he's in the right location. It's like whoever took the photo stood where he is standing now. Then he spots a bench across the road from the gates and he heads there so he can gather his wits and decide how he's going to proceed. It's crazy what he's doing. He feels for the letter in his pocket. He thinks about what he's written. It's addressed to the girl: Amber O'Connor. He's never written a letter before so it's more a note in his best not-joined-up writing.

'I'm really sorry for what happened to your da.' That's how he starts it. 'And I'm really sorry for your ma. I didn't think anything like that could happen. I was there. I'm sorry. And I'm sorry for you too.'

He doesn't use the ma's name.

There are two seagulls standing on the bench. They're squawking at each other like they're bickering about something. He shoos them off and sits. He pulls the baseball cap low over his forehead and buttons his jacket. There's a breeze about.

A bell rings inside the building and within seconds there's a burst of activity. He's only noticing now the line of cars parked on the road up the side of the school and these suddenly spurt to life like they need to be somewhere fast once they collect their crew. The front doors of the school spring open and a herd of girls bursts through, noisy, in a hurry to be gone. They carry bags and bottles of water and their jumpers in their hands, and some sprint towards the cars and disappear inside but most spill out through the gate and he scans them for a face he's hoping to recognise.

This is madness what he's doing. Why does he need to see the girl? All he has to do is post the letter in the school letterbox.

He pulls the cap tighter against his scalp as the teachers' cars make their careful exit. He hopes he doesn't look like a perv. He can hardly see anyone now because two girls have decided to stand in front of him as they peer at something on a phone.

'Hey!' he shouts and they turn to frown at him. 'Yiz're blockin' me light!'

They stare at him and then at the sky like they don't know what he's talking about, but they move because he's putting out a fuck-off vibe.

But the stream of bodies has ended and now it's just the four or five cars that are still parked in the car park along with his two seagulls swooping for crumbs. He feels for the letter in his pocket and squeezes the envelope. Where is the letterbox? He thought it might be near the gates, but there's no sign of anything resembling one. It must be in by the school doors. What if there's no letterbox and letters get given to the school secretary? He stands up and feels his courage melting fast.

A squad car passes along the main road that's to the side of him. There are two cops in the car and he's sure the cop in the passenger seat gave him the evil eye. Has someone in the school seen him hanging round outside and called them? They must think he's perving school kids. He sits back down on the seat and scrolls through his phone like he's stopped here to read a text or better still answer one. Then he thinks he sees the squad car flash by in the other direction. Is it the same squad car or is it a different one? What are the chances of two squad cars going by practically one after the other? Maybe it wasn't a squad car, but he can't be certain. He needs to get off the road. He peers off to the side and notices there's a church just up from where he is. That's where he can hide. He'll go there for ten minutes or so until the coast is clear.

His feet take him along the footpath and towards the big metal gates of the church. The gate is locked but there's two smaller gates on either side and they're open. There's a car park inside the gate with spaces for six cars. Only two of them are taken. One of the cars is a black Volkswagen Golf and the other is a blue Hyundai Tucson, five years old but looking like it's well cared for.

Camry, Prius, Chevrolet Silverado ...

The words invade his brain but he can't remember the rest of the list. It's good that he's forgetting.

He wants to stop to admire the Golf but keeps walking. He does pause, though, when he sees that the left rear wheel is flat. He turns towards the church door and notices now that there's a pathway down the side of the church that leads to a small building that's attached to it. A sign points towards it saying 'Parish Centre'. It has a large front window looking out to sea. The front door opens and a woman is coming out. He doesn't want to be seen here, so he hurries on and enters the church.

He hasn't been inside a church since he made his confo, or maybe he was there once or twice afterwards. He doesn't really like churches because they remind him of his da's funeral and sitting on his ma's lap in the front row, too frozen to let in what had really happened and crying because his ma was bawling her eyes out.

He stands and gazes up towards the altar with the two large stain-glass windows behind it spilling red and orange sunlight onto it. He glances to his right and there's a small table with leaflets on it. There's a notice board above it with a poster of another church and looking for names for an upcoming trip to Knock. There are about ten names scribbled already with phone numbers attached. Beside the table is a kind of press with what looks like a bronze letterbox cut into the top of it with the word 'Offerings' on a sign screwed into the wood just above it.

He can post the letter here! The girl will still get it because it has the school's name on it as well as hers. He looks about him and then takes the envelope from his pocket. He pushes it quickly into the letterbox before he has time to change his mind. This is better than going to the school. Like, what was he thinking? This is a better idea and if nobody knows where to deliver the letter then it's not his problem. And he can tell Jackie he's dropped off the letter and she'll say she's proud of him. He wants her to be proud of him.

He needs to wait another few minutes, though, before going back out. But what if someone were to come into the church now and see him there – loitering like he's gonna rob the place? He could pretend he's here to light some candles. He could even do that.

He glances to his left and sees a stand like a little terrace where the candles are. There's four lit already. He suddenly realises he's wearing his baseball cap and now he hears his ma's voice telling him to take it off. He obeys the voice. He can't believe how quiet the place is when there's nobody in it. It's peaceful even. Now he's remembering his ma lighting candles on his birthday cake and telling him to make a wish. Are the candles here to let people make wishes? But now he hears Jackie's voice in his head telling him to light one – and be humble enough to ask for forgiveness. He's feeling like a fool, like an eejit. That must mean he's humble.

He reads the notice. It tells him he can put his money offering in the slot nearby, but there's no prices given, like it's up to himself, like maybe it's a test to see how mean he is. He searches in his pocket for change but he fishes out two twenty-cent pieces and a fiver. Fuck! He can't just light a candle for forty cents. That would be some sort of insult.

But a fiver! That's a whole lot of money to spend on a wish when he could probably get more value from a couple of scratch cards.

He holds the fiver in his hand, not ready to let go of it yet. He could make a wish to get Sharon back. Then he thinks of Tina. What's that about? How can he make a wish involving Sharon and be thinking of a different girl who probably doesn't need anything from him? Has he even asked for forgiveness yet? But he's posted the letter. That's the main thing. Now he need only light his candle and a big wishy prayer and then get the hell back on the bus into town.

'Are you OK?' a woman's voice says behind him and he jumps with the fright she gives him. 'Oh sorry, did I scare you? I'm so sorry.'

He turns. It's her! Your one, Georgina! The mother of your one, Amber. He wants to slap his cap back on his head but it's too late. She's gazing at him suspiciously. He holds his breath, waiting for her to scream and then run from the church like a mad one, like she's just met the devil himself. She must know him. She must sense who he is. He lowers his face so she can't see his eyes. What's she doing here? Well, she does live out here, of course, but ... what the fuck is going on? Is this because he's thinking of making a wishy washy wish like he's at some fountain rather than asking for forgiveness?

'Do you need change?' she says, and she nods towards his fiver. 'That's an expensive candle.'

She smiles, and he knows now she doesn't recognise him. How could she? He was gone before she got to the body. He glances at her and then looks down to the fiver in his fingers.

'Naw, it's all right. I just have to make a prayer for my ... my da.'

'Oh, he died then?'

'A long time ago.'

'That's a very nice thing you're doing. You must miss him?'

'Yeah. I do.'

What the fuck? Where were all these words coming from? Lighting a candle for his da? Now he's really screwing things up. He's meant to be lighting a candle to get Sharon back. And he's suddenly got a picture of yer one Tina in his head with her angel face on her. What the fuck? How come he's not thinking of lighting one for this woman and her daughter? Isn't that what Jackie would have wanted him to do? Isn't it what Sharon would like him to do also? Is this the reason the woman has suddenly materialised like some sort of messed-up miracle? And now that he's mentioned his da he'd better light a candle for him too because what would his da think of him if he can't do that much in his memory? Bad enough he's missed his anniversary Mass. And what about Vinnie? Isn't he the one he needs the most help with so he can figure out what he's up to and then get clear of him? At this rate he'll have the church on fire with candles. He feels like running from the place. But he can't do that or she'll think he's trying to rob the candle money. He glances at her once more.

She's a little different from the photo. Her hair is a little greyer, like she's letting it go that way and not bothering to dye it like his ma does. There are frown lines on her forehead and dark patches under her sad-looking eyes.

'I'm lighting a candle for my husband,' she says.

'He died?'

'Yeah. And I'll do one for my daughter as well.'

'She's not …'

'Oh no,' she says and laughs. 'I'm just lighting a candle for her so she'll do well in her tests. New school – so she needs to impress.'

'Oh, OK,' Joey says, and he slips the fiver into the slot and selects two candles, not sure now who the fuck they belong to. He plucks out a lit one and then uses it to light the two he's chosen. He can see the woman out of the corner of his eye light two of her own. She sets them down beside one another. Then she picks out a fiver from her purse.

'I hope I didn't set the rate,' Joey says, nodding towards the money.

She laughs as she folds it and pushes it through the slot.

'I'm sorry!' he says. 'I'm sorry … for … what I did … I mean … for scaring you.'

She turns to stare at him like she doesn't know what he means and then she smiles. 'No! You're fine. It was me gave you a fright, as I remember, not the other way round. Good luck with your wishes and sorry again about your dad.'

She moves away from him and goes to sit in one of the pews. He watches her as she blesses herself. She sits still for a couple of seconds before getting to her feet and making her way to the door.

'Bye,' she calls back to him.

Joey waves at her, then leans against the side of the metal shelf that holds the candles. He can feel his head spin and he's afraid he's going to fall. He goes to the pew and sits where the woman sat. He closes his eyes and gets a smell in his nostrils like it's one of Jackie's scented candles. It's nicer, not as overpowering, and he knows it's the scent the woman has left in her wake.

'Excuse me!'

It's her voice again. He opens his eyes and twists his head round towards the door. She's standing there and her frown is even more noticeable. 'Sorry to disturb you, but would you know how to fix a flat tyre?'

Joey gets to his feet immediately and walks towards her.

'That's no problem. The Golf is yours, then?'

'Oh, you saw it?'

'Yeah. It's a lovely car.'

'Do you mind? Like, have you got the time? I would ask Father Frank but his back is playing up on him.'

'It's OK, I've loads of time.'

'And your good deed will add to your candles. Whatever you prayed for has to come true.'

Joey smiles at her and follows her out. He doesn't know what to feel. He wants to help her but he also knows he just wants to make a run for it, sprint all the way back into town and not bother with a bus.

The boot of the car is open and the spare tyre and jack and wrench are all waiting for him beside the flat wheel.

'I'd try and do it myself but I got my nails done this morning and I know I'd destroy them.'

She shows him the back of her hand and he sees the plain gold ring beside two others that sparkle. There's a shine off the red nail varnish she's showing him and the nails are a decent length and not like the daggers that Sharon wears when she's heading out on the town.

He sets to work and he suddenly feels nervous about kneeling beside a car. But he tells himself it's different this time. He's not stealing. He's putting something back in place. He's here to help. He quickly loosens the nuts and then jacks the car up. He can feel her eyes on him.

'I'm watching what you do so I can learn. My daughter gives out to me for not doing this sort of thing myself.'

Joey wipes his forehead with the back of his hand and then turns to smile up at her. What is she thinking? How is she feeling? Does she have nightmares like he does? Does she have to take medication? And what about her daughter?

'Amber!' he says. Oh my God, he's said it aloud.

'What?'

'Am ...ver ... am very used to changing tyres ... so no worries about that.' He rubs his cheek with the back of his hand so he can hide the blood rushing to his face.

'I thought you said "Amber".'

'Amber?'

'That's the name of my daughter.'

'Nice.' He gives his cheeks another rub. He keeps his eyes down. He doesn't speak. And she doesn't speak either and he's grateful for it. Amber! What the fuck was he thinking?

'Oh, you're here,' she says to someone behind him and when he looks up, he can see the girl in school uniform give her mother a hug. And then she's staring down at him where he kneels palming on the hubcap.

'Hey, Amber! This is … hey, I don't know your name?' she says.

Joey squints up at the mother then at Amber.

'Joseph. My name is Joseph,' he says.

The girl looks away from him, uninterested. 'I'm not going home with you, Mum. I'm meeting some of the girls down at the shop.'

'That's OK,' she says. 'But I want you home by six for your dinner.'

Amber doesn't linger to make any more conversation but turns on her heels and strides away and is lost from sight behind the car. 'And you've got studying to do,' her mother shouts after her. Then her attention comes back to Joey and she pulls out her purse.

'Hey, no way,' Joey says. 'If I take money off you, then I lose the extra benefit with the candles.'

The woman laughs as she puts her purse away. Then she walks back towards the office at the side and turns a key in the door. She's coming back towards him; then she stops and turns and speaks to someone. A man in black clothes comes into view and stops to chat to her. He has a balding head of grizzly grey hair and a beard to match. There's something familiar about him, though it might be he's the spit of yer man Davos from *Game of Thrones*. They speak like they know each other well, and then he can see Georgina point towards her car. They're talking about him, he's sure. He turns his head away. He lifts the flat tyre and places it snugly in the boot as their footsteps approach.

'This is Father Frank,' Georgina says. 'And this is Joseph. The young man who has arrived like an angel to rescue me.'

The priest puts out his hand and Joey shakes it. The hand is warm and firm.

'Do you live around here, Joseph?' the priest asks and Joey detects a hint of suspicion in the man's voice. And there's a hint of it also in Georgina's eyes.

'No! I live in town. I was just out this way like to … I don't know, just to go for a walk by the sea. And then I came in here. Like, my aunt wanted me to light candles for her.'

'For her as well as your dad?' Georgina asks.

'She can make a fiver go a long way,' Joey says, and the pair of them laugh at this.

'Well, I'm glad you did come in and I got a chance to meet you,' Georgina says. 'And I hope you get everything you prayed for.'

'He was praying?' Father Frank says, surprised. 'My God, maybe we have a boy that's got the call.'

Joey makes a pretend laugh. Georgina's laugh sounds more sincere.

'Well, I have to go now, father,' she says. 'I've locked up and everything is in order with the accounts.' She looks at Joey.

'And father Frank will give you a lift into town. Won't you, Father?'

'Of course. The least I can do.'

Father Frank thanks her and then he unlocks the gate and they watch her get into her car and drive off.

Joey isn't sure how to feel.

'You're not the only angel,' Father Frank says.

'What?'

'That woman is like a gift that was sent.'

'Yeah?'

'Yeah, she had her own business but gave it all up to come work for me.'

'She seems really nice,' Joey says. Then he pats the knees of his jeans and puts on his jacket, ready to leave.

'I don't mind getting the bus, Father,' he says, wanting to be shot of the place.

'I can't allow that, after your good deed. Anyway I'm heading that way.'

He presses his car fob and the light blinks and then he goes to the passenger side and opens the door like he's going to be Joey's chauffeur.

19

'Were you a Mass server?'

'Do I look like one?'

'I can't say you do.'

'I did serve Mass once when I was in primary school but the priest wasn't too impressed with me.'

'Why not?'

'I drank some altar wine before the Mass started and then I fell asleep.'

Father Frank laughs.

'You know your way around cars?'

'Yeah.'

'Your dad?'

'Yeah, something like that.'

'You want to be a mechanic?'

'I don't know. Maybe.'

They go from one set of traffic lights to the next in silence, but when they stop for red, the priest sees it like question time.

'You're not in college then?'

'No. I work in a shop in town. But I want to get something better at some stage.'

'Well good for you.'

The lights change and they drive once more in silence. Joey is a little nervous. He's not sure if it's because of all the questions or because the priest is a shite driver.

There's a pair of glasses in the well beside the gear stick and he's tempted to suggest the priest use them. But he thinks it might be an insult, especially when the guy is doing him a favour – not that he wants any favours from a priest.

'You can let me out here, first place you can pull into,' Joey says when he sees the Five Lamps up ahead of him.

Father Frank pulls in and Joey unclasps the seat belt. He's ready to escape when he feels the man's fingers on his elbow.

'Just a second, Joseph.'

Joey turns. 'There's nothing I need to be worried about, is there? Regarding Georgie … and her daughter?'

Joey is afraid to open his mouth because he's not sure what might escape. He extends his hand to open the door, but the priest's fingers are still there at his elbow. Joey turns to look at the hand.

'You're not one of *those* priests, are yeh?'

The priest removes his fingers.

'I wasn't trying to rob you, if that's what she said.'

'She said no such thing.'

'In fact, I gave you money. A fiver for two measly candles.'

Father Frank laughs. 'You know those candles are a great money earner. I should put in more of them.'

Joey goes to move but he feels a gentle touch on his sleeve this time.

'The question still stands. Do I need to be worried? Georgie got spooked when you mentioned her daughter's name.'

'I mentioned her daughter's name?'

'She's convinced you did. Well did you?'

Joey doesn't answer. He stares at the narrowed eyes that are gazing at him like they can see right through him. 'She said she got a feeling that your presence has something to do with something that's happened to her ... to them ... in the past.'

'A feeling?'

'That's what she said. She didn't feel threatened – just spooked.'

'I haven't met her daughter before. I haven't met either of them before now,' he says, not exactly lying to the priest. 'So you've nothing to be worried about. And neither does she ... or her daughter.'

'That's good to hear, Joseph. You go now and mind yourself.'

'And talking of spooked, you need to wear those glasses when you're driving,' Joey says as he opens the door and steps out onto the street.

20

The two boys are there on their scooters. They're not even trying to disguise the fact they're following him.

He plans to take the green line Luas from Marlborough heading southside, even though it isn't where he wants to go. There's one of the boys down one end of the platform and what looks like his twin down the other end.

The Luas tram glides in and the warning bell rings and he hesitates, watchful as people get off and spill around him. He steps on and turns to see the pair of them quickly fold their scooters and enter the tram just before the doors slide shut.

He stands just inside the door with his elbow level with the emergency button. They stand, a carriage length away, eyeing him from inside their hoodie tops, waiting for his next move.

When the door opens at Ranelagh, he waits as one gang of noisy schoolchildren enters and another gang exits, then he melts out just before the doors slide shut.

On the platform he turns and sees one of the boys locked in on the other side of the door as the Luas takes him away. He shows the boy his middle finger. He turns and sees the other boy is out. He's behind him but struggling to get his scooter past the student group. Joey swivels on his feet and runs towards the stairs that lead down to the street.

He sees a girl ahead of him. She's gotten off the Luas also and is already hurrying down the steps. He recognises her immediately. Tina!

He takes the stairs two at a time and when he reaches the street he turns right and sees her a few shopfronts up ahead of him. He turns to look back but there's no sign of the scooter head.

He quickens his step and he's right behind her when she turns abruptly and enters what looks like a café. He hurries and reaches it before the door can swing shut. There's a window on the top half of the door with a square of white curtain. There's a small sign there that says 'Closed'.

He ignores the sign and goes inside. She hears him behind her and turns.

'Tina!' he says at the same time she calls out 'Joey!'

'What are you doing here?' she says, then turns towards the kitchen area where they can hear loud Italian voices. Her attention is back to him as she waits for an answer.

'I saw you when I got off the Luas and I just wanted to talk to you … to see what you're … I dunno … what you're up to.'

She holds her hands out to indicate where she is.

'You're Italian?' he says like it's just dawned on him. How come he didn't notice the look or the accent before this? 'I love the T-shirt, by the way.'

It's black with a seagull posing on the front of it, chest like a bodybuilder, with a slice of salami pizza sticking out of its yellow beak.

'You should go before my father comes out and I've to explain –'

'That's your da I hear in there?'

'Yes. And my mother also.'

It's like mentioning their names conjures them up because the door to the kitchen swings open and a tall, wide load of a man with short curly grey hair comes through. He stops at the sight of Joey.

'Who is this?' he asks.

'Papa this is Joey. He's from … Trinity.'

'Ah, Trinity! One of your smart friends,' he says, extending his hand towards Joey. Joey takes it and feels the firm grip. He is anxious to know where the hoodie has gone.

'I just bumped into him,' Tina is saying, 'as he was coming off the Luas, and he wanted to see our café.'

'It's really class looking. I must come and eat here some time,' Joey says.

'Yes! Yes!' Tina's father says, and then he rattles off a load of sentences in Italian and Tina looks offended and says something back to him that he snorts at, and then he's gone back into the kitchen.

'I have to go, Joey. I have to work.'

Joey goes towards the door and pushes the tiny curtain aside. The scooter head is across the road talking into his phone. Joey closes the curtain.

'What's going on, Joey?'

'Ah nothing really. There was a guy on the Luas with an electric scooter and he bumped into me and I told him where he could stuff it. But then the little fucker gets off at the same stop as me and heads after me like he wants to do me damage.'

'Oh my God, Joey, that was scary.'

'Yeah, so lucky I spotted you and could give him the slip. You saved me from getting into a scrap.' Tina goes to the door and opens it and stands outside and checks the street. 'I see him,' she says. 'He's moving away up towards the village, so you're okay to go, Joey, once you're not going that way.'

Joey goes to stand beside her. He peers out, then gets distracted by her presence, like he'd rather stay and talk some more to her instead of having to make a run for it. She becomes aware that he's gazing at her.

'What?' she says.

'Nothing! Just, it's nice to be here, that's all. And what was your auld fella saying to you? Was he giving out about you bringing me in here?'

'No! He'd just prefer if I gave up art school and worked here full-time. He doesn't think much of my career plans.'

'He's not as big a fan of your T-shirts as I am.'

'I do more than T-shirts,' she says, like she's offended. 'I do badges and posters, and cards.'

'I can imagine.'

'Would you like a job here?'

'Me?'

'Yes. You! Would you like a job in the kitchen?'

'A job? You're kidding me.'

'I'm not. We're short-staffed.'

'A job here?'

'Yes, but in the kitchen.'

'Washing up?'

'And prepping some of the food.'

'Cooking?'

'Jesus, Joey! Not at the start.'

'Fucking hell that would be amazing.' He beams her a smile as he says it.

He opens the door and leans his head out to peer up the road. There's no sign of the hoodie.

'I'll come back and talk to you about that offer,' he says. He opens the door fully, then stops and turns to her once more. 'Sharon?'

'She's OK. I haven't seen much of her, though.'

He nods. Her eyes are a beautiful brown, the colour of chestnuts, and her lips are full and red. She looks away.

'I'm going to sort all my shit out and then I'll come back and talk to you. Yeah?'

'Goodbye, Joey,' she says, like she doesn't believe him.

And then he's gone and sprinting down the footpath and up the steps to the Luas platform where he'll get the tram out to the northside of the city where he hopes to find Vinnie.

21

Joey doesn't know as much about bikes as he does about cars, but he's certain it was a Honda Steed VCL 400cc that Vinnie rode. And he found it easily enough on Done Deal with the twin silver cylinders at the side and the distinctive little back rest for the pillion passenger. It's a 1996 model with 41,000km on the clock. Joey doesn't ever want to own a bike, but he likes looking at them. And somewhere he remembers a friend of his ma's giving him a backer up and down the street in front of his house. The asking price for Vinnie's bike is €2800 and 'no messers or time wasters need apply'. That's Vinnie's lingo all right.

When he rang the number, it wasn't Vinnie who replied, but a guy who told him where he needed to go. The area is called Grangegorman, a place Joey has never heard of let alone set foot in before.

When he eventually gets there, he feels like a stranger in a new city. There's been a mad load of building going on. And when he sees the college, he wishes he could be a student like Sharon and meet all these interesting heads like Miles and Rodney. But then he'd probably have to put up with the likes of Bernice too. He thinks of Sharon, the way she talks about Trinity. He doesn't blame her for not wanting him to mess it up on her. But he doesn't know what he'd have to do to go to a place like this. He'd have to start reading books and doing exams and there's no space in his head to even think about all that stuff.

He turns his back on all the new builds and uses his phone to guide him away towards the warren of side streets until he sees the bike shop. He puts the phone away.

It's more like a lock-up than a shop. Two grey steel doors are open and the space between them has four bikes for sale. One of them is the Honda. He knows he's in the right place and he feels his chest tighten like he has to remind himself to breathe. The weather is dry and warm, and there's work going on in the small yard to the front of the building. There's a guy in sleeveless grey overalls who seems to be working on an old Honda 50 while another guy with a black grizzly beard and battered blue lumberjack shirt sits in a green plastic garden chair smoking a rollie and talking to the guy working on the Honda. He looks up when he sees Joey.

'Who do I talk to about the Honda Steed?' Joey says and the man points his oily thumb behind him.

'That'd be The Vee you'd be needing. He's back there somewhere if you wanna search.'

It's a deeper cave of a building than he imagined. There's full bikes and bits of bikes all scattered about, with spare parts and exhausts hanging from racks on each wall. There's a table covered in old newspapers with oily-looking chains laid out on them. Beside those exhibits are motorbike magazines and three dirty-looking mugs, and a plate with a half-eaten toastie of some sort on it. Off to one side there's a pool table that's dabbed with greasy fingerprints but in working order from the balls that are spilled on it. Then he sees the stairs behind leading up into an office that's on stilts and has a large window looking out over the workshop.

He goes to the stairs and climbs up. He can hear music now from inside the office. It's a Rory Gallagher track from *On The Boards*. He shakes his head and almost smiles as the memory hits him of Vinnie playing the CD in one of the old bangers he borrowed from Quinlan's garage.

He knocks and hears some sort of call out in response and opens the door. Vinnie is sitting in an old office chair at a desk that's neat and tidy looking. The office is as neat as the desk with very little in it except for a leather couch that has a glass-topped coffee table in front of it. Vinnie is writing something in a hard-backed A4-sized notebook and he turns and smiles when he sees Joey standing there, staring at him. He grabs at a remote and the music retreats and becomes barely audible.

'Took your time to work it out!' Vinnie says by way of greeting.

Joey waits by the door. Vinnie is wearing black jeans and black slip-on boots. There's a slit cut into one of the knees and it reminds him of Bernice and her creations. The thought sends blood racing to his cheeks.

'For fucksake come in,' Vinnie says, as he closes the notebook and goes to the glass-topped table and takes up a packet of smokes.

'You were supposed to go and talk to Quinlan,' Joey says.

Vinnie eyes him and shakes his head and laughs. 'Will you sit down, Joey, and don't be causing a draught.'

Joey pushes the door shut but stands where he is.

'Sit down,' Vinnie growls, pointing to the leather couch as he goes back to his office chair and sits into it and lights up a cigarette. He's wearing a long-sleeved green T-shirt with the sleeves rolled up to where they become stuck like bandages on his new show-off muscle lumps. He has his hair tied back in a ponytail, like he's been getting grooming tips off Big Richie. He points the box at Joey.

Joey shakes his head and goes to the couch and sits. He rests his hands on his knees and looks at Vinnie like he's waiting for an explanation.

'What?' Vinnie says.

'You told me you'd talk to Quinlan about his car!'

'Sorry, Joey. I didn't think it was that important.'

'He wants it back! And anything that was in it when you took off that time.'

'The car was a piece of junk.'

'Yeah, but he wants it back.'

Vinnie chuckles like he's enjoying the conversation more than Joey is.

'I told you already – I sold it. But why's he hassling you about it? Is he hassling you?'

Joey wants to tell him the truth. He wants to tell him that he's not only hassling him but he's bringing Jackie and Sharon into it also. But he can't say the words because he remembers Ginsey lying on the road and the wet patch on his tracksuit bottoms.

'No!'

'Cos if he is, I can do something about it. I know where his family live. And they're not protected like they think they are.'

'There's no need for that! Like … he just came into the shop to buy smokes. That was all. And he asked about you – said he had unfinished business with you, and it was Weso who told me he was bad-mouthing you about the car.'

'Don't be listening to that little tosser.'

'But why are you hiding out here, then?'

'I'm not hiding.'

'Well, if you're not, why didn't you tell Ma you were back – or Jackie?'

'Because they're pissed off with me too, just like you seem to be.'

'But they don't know what you did … we did?'

'I didn't leave on good terms with either of them. And both of them know that something bad must have happened because of the way I left.'

'Well, I didn't tell them anything!'

He remembers how he nearly spilled his guts to Jackie and he feels his face go red once more. Fucksake! He'll have to get something like Botox if this shit with his face keeps happening. Vinnie pulls on his cigarette then stares down at his feet and blows smoke like to cover them.

He shakes his head and Joey knows that Vinnie doesn't want to talk about what happened.

'How you getting on with Jackie?'

'Fine!'

'I was going to make contact with her – but I heard that you're in there with her and she's got a guy in tow and has found religion. And then I figured she didn't need me to complicate her life. Sounds like she's doing good. Yeah?'

'Yeah. And the new guy she's with … he's …'

'What? Is he not nice to her?'

'No! He's grand. He's a real gentleman, in fact. I like him and she seems to … you know … she likes him from what I can see. She's joining his choir – a church choir he has, so she must like him if she's doing that.'

'No way!'

'Yeah, that's what she told me.'

Vinnie kinda chuckles to himself at the idea of that. 'You know I used be in a choir in primary school.'

'You in school? How come I can't picture that? Unless it was like a school in that film of yer man Fagan with the ugly dog.'

Vinnie laughs like he enjoys the joke.

Joey didn't mean it as a joke. He lets his gaze wander round the room. He sees boxes like the one he saw in Isabel's bedroom.

'You're not really selling dodgy boxes? Are yeh?' Vinnie turns to eye the shelves.

'Yeah, I'm going legit!'

Joey can't stop himself from letting out a chuckle.

'What? You don't believe me?'

'Dodgy boxes aren't legit!'

'Yeah, but they're next door to it. And that's good enough for me. Yeah?'

'Yeah, if you say so.'

'I do say so. And I've the perfect place here to operate from.'

Joey doesn't see any sign of living quarters in the building and he wonders where Vinnie is staying when he's not working. But he doesn't really want to know. Not yet anyway. Not until he's sure about what if anything he's up to.

'All I'm trying to do now, Joey, is keep my head down and do some work and save some money. Turn over a new leaf, like. And maybe in six months' time everybody might be willing to see me in a different light – especially when I've a load of dosh. And when that happens, I'll try and sort out a decent apartment to live in, so you and Isabel can come round and stay. Yeah?'

Joey doesn't know whether to believe him or not. Can it be true he knows nothing about Quinlan looking for him? Sharon told Joey he has to find Vinnie and get him to stay away or he'll never be able to win her back. That means he should tell Vinnie everything that's happened. He should definitely tell him about the cop. He should tell him about Jackie's injured finger and Sharon's stolen laptop. He should tell him about Rodney getting beaten up, and about the scooter heads who are following him everywhere he goes. And he could tell him how Sharon has broken up with him and it's Vinnie's fault for coming back and ruining everything on him. But he knows if he tells him any of this, then Vinnie will surely go and hunt out those scooter heads and probably get into some serious shit with Quinlan that will involve the cops and probably send him on the run again or have him end up in prison. Joey can't bear the thought of that on his conscience along with everything else. There has to be another way to get Quinlan off his back.

'For fucksake, Joey, just because I'm around doesn't have to mean there's trouble brewing.'

Joey stares at him, like he's wondering how he's now able to read his mind. Or maybe he's reading the look on his face, or is it the fact he's gone all quiet?

'Like what the fuck would have happened to you,' Vinnie says, 'if I hadn't been out in your estate the other night? And I do that most nights.'

'Do what?'

'I take a spin out on the bike and drive past your ma's house. You know, just to make sure everything is OK out there. And I go past Sharon's gaff too.'

Joey tries to imagine the noise of Vinnie driving through the estate and feels sorry for him. Does he think he's Batman or some other sort of vigilante crusader?

'Sharon's laptop got stolen,' he blurts out.

'On the estate?'

'No! In town.'

'When?'

'Just the other day.'

'And she didn't get it back?'

'Not a hope.' It's a lie, and he hopes his face isn't betraying him. But it just occurs to him now, maybe, just maybe, if he plays this right, he might get Vinnie to hand over that other laptop – that's if he still has it.

'That's shit,' Vinnie says.

'Yeah. Everything she had was on it. All her essays and stuff. Now she needs to get another one. I said I'd help her out.'

'There's no need for that.'

'Why not?'

'Because I have a laptop I can give her.'

Yes!

'Once she's not too choosy about the appearance – though she can't be worried about that kinda stuff or she wouldn't be hanging with you.'

Joey shows him his middle finger, then turns away and peers at the shelf unit at the back of the room that's stacked with all sorts of crap like bits that could be parts of engines or some sort of art pieces. There's manuals and box files, greasy with fingerprints, but all look organised like they could be in a library. But it's the space between the shelf unit and the ceiling that Vinnie is eyeing. He goes to the unit and reaches up to take down an expensive-looking black laptop bag. He hands it to Joey.

'Is this the one belonging to Quinlan? That was in the boot of that car?'

'Yeah, and it's a piece of crap, like the car."

'Don't you want to keep it?'

'No. Can't stand the yokes. I was thinking of selling it, but there's a bit of a crack in the corner of the screen. So let Sharon have it. She can get the screen replaced if she's that fussy about it.'

Joey places the bag on the glass table and kneels down beside it.

'That fancy bag came with it. I've lost the charger. But she can buy herself one.'

Joey zips it open and pulls out the laptop. It's old and scratched. He opens the lid and the screen has a spider-web crack in one corner and he wonders now if it's even working.

'So, Quinlan's pissed off because I took that car of his? Jesus, talk about hatching a grudge.'

'What if you just offered to pay him back what you got for the car? Like, that would put an end to it.'

'Not going to happen, Joey.' Then Vinnie reaches into his jacket pocket that's hanging from the back of his chair and takes out his wallet.

'I don't need money,' Joey says. 'I have a job.'

'I'm not giving you money.' He pulls out a card and hands it to Joey. It's a business card and it has 'Vin' written on it with a mobile number at the bottom of it. 'You take that and keep it safe. And if there's any shit going down and you need my help then just send me a text and I'll come running. OK?'

Joey stares at the card, smiles at Vinnie, then puts it in his pocket.

'I'll activate the bat signal,' he says.

Vinnie smiles at him like he could be Robin and things are back the way they used to be.

'Now how about me and you, bud, going out for a sandwich? There's a little coffee shop just round the corner that those fuckin' students haven't discovered yet. They do a nice cappuccino and those Danish pastries you used to like. Or they could do you a chicken and stuffing sandwich? No?'

Joey is hungry and the thought of the sandwich is tempting, but he's not sure if he wants to spend any more time talking to Vinnie. He knows his stepda is keen to hear all the news about Jackie and Ma, but Joey isn't ready for that yet. He's not ready to chat and be called 'bud' like nothing ever happened. Not yet anyway. Not until he can sort out what's going on or find out if he's been lied to.

'Sorry, Vinnie, but I have to get back to do a shift in the shop,' he says, and he can actually see the look of disappointment in his stepda's eyes. But what the fuck. He has to be careful this time. And now that he has the laptop maybe he can sort all of this shit out himself.

22

He's on the Luas back to town with the laptop bag held firmly when his phone rings. The number is withheld so he's not sure if he should answer it. But he does.

He doesn't recognise the accent immediately. It's Rodney.

'How did you get my number?' is the first thing he wants to know.

'I got it from Stephen.'

What's going on? Why is the guy ringing him unless it's to look for some sort of apology? And for Sharon's sake he doesn't mind giving him one.

'Hey, I'm sorry for what happened to you the other night,' he begins to say.

'I'm not calling about that,' Rodney interrupts him.

Joey is relieved. The guy's voice sounds OK and maybe he didn't get a bad beating after all. Maybe it was just Miles and Sharon making more of it than was necessary – just to make their point.

'I'm calling about Sharon.'

Joey can feel his breath shorten and there's a lurch down at the pit of his stomach.

'What about Sharon?'

'She's gone from the apartment.'

He thinks of those scooter heads and is afraid to ask what they've done to her.

'What do you mean – gone?'

'I mean she's packed most of her stuff and she's gone home.'

'What?'

'Yeah. Herself and Bernice got into a blaze of a row.'

'Was it about what happened to you?'

'No! They were talking about ... Botox, I think, to start with. Bernice was going on about women using it and Sharon said she thinks anyone who gets it done must be feeling pretty shit about themselves. Then Miles rapidly changed the subject by talking about the book he's reading. But then doesn't Bernice come straight out and says that Sharon sounds like someone out of a Roddy Doyle novel. Sharon then gets all spikey with her and tells her if she has a problem with how she speaks she could go an' shite. And she should record her own voice sometime and she'd soon hear the poison underneath all the sugar.'

'Ah, for fucksake!'

'Yeah, but that wasn't all.'

'What? Did Sharon, like, dig her one?'

'No, better than that – she told Bernice that everything about her was fake and she should call herself "Ber" from now on and drop the "nice" bit because there was nothing fucking nice about her.'

'Sharon said that?'

'Yeah!'

'Fair play to her!'

'OK, but it didn't end there.'

'Why, what did she do then?'

'She didn't do or say anything, but Miles laughed. No, sorry, he "smirked" at what Sharon said and then Bernice lost it completely with him. He said he didn't smirk. He might have just smiled, but she said it was a smirk and what was he doing studying English in Trinity if he didn't even know the difference between a smirk and a smile.'

'He smirked?' Joey says. 'What the fuck is wrong with that?'

'A lot, according to Bernice. She gets her phone out and Googles the meaning of the word and then she reads it out to him so he can see clearly why she was so upset with him – and he's starting to get miffed now, even though it's hard to make him annoyed. And he tells her again he didn't smirk, and even if he did she probably deserved it because you don't ask someone to change their accent just because you don't like the sound of it. So, then Bernice has a total meltdown. She storms off and swears she wants nothing more to do with Miles ever again. The poor fella is devastated over it. And Sharon thinks it's all her fault. I told Miles this is all about Bernice being jealous of the way me and him get on so well with Sharon. And I told Sharon the same but she doesn't want to believe that's the reason.'

'So, she's gone home for a break?'

'No! She said she's finished with college.'

'Ah, for fucksake.'

He wants to lower the phone and end the call because his mind is in a whirl.

'You still there, Joseph?'

'Yeah – and fucksake, it's Joey!'

'OK, Joey! I rang her but there's no answer. She must have her phone switched off. I want to call to her mother's place but I don't know where she lives. And there's more of her stuff here.'

'Leave it there!' Joey snaps. Fuckers must want her out badly.

'No, it's not that. If I bring it out to her it's like an excuse to go see her – to talk to her, get her to come back.'

'Where are you now?' Joey asks.

'I'm in the apartment but I can meet you if you want to show me where she lives.'

'I can give you her address.'

'Yeah, you could, but I'd prefer if you came with me – you know, to show I've gotten over what happened and there's no bad blood between me and you.'

'Yeah, OK,' Joey says, 'but you leave her stuff there where it is.'

23

They hardly talk on the way out and Joey walks fast from the Luas stop. It's still bright but he can feel the darkness descending. He can hear Rodney struggle to keep up with his pace. He slows down a bit, remembering that the lad took a beating and he's to blame for that too.

They tripped him up, Rodney, and then kicked him like for fun. He has bruising round his right eye and he says his arms are sore from where he tried to protect his head. His stomach is sore too, but he seems happy not to talk about it. Joey is happy not to talk about it also. He has other things on his mind. He has the computer bag on his shoulder. He still hasn't had the time to get a charger to see if the thing is even working and if it contains info that's causing Quinlan's freak-out.

Sharon opens the door, scowls, and immediately turns to walk back into the house.

'She didn't shut the door in our faces,' Rodney says in a whisper. 'That's something at least.'

'Yeah,' Joey says, as he leads the way down the shadowy hallway towards the light in the kitchen.

The house is quiet. Sharon has retreated into the kitchen, where she likes to sit. She's sitting there now at the table with her laptop open in front of her and an episode of *Gilmore Girls* playing that he knows she's seen millions of times before. She's put her earphones in, like she wants to block out all talk.

Joey pulls out the chair that's across from her and sits on it. Rodney stands near the doorway like he's waiting for permission to come closer. Joey says nothing, just watches her. She sighs and lowers the lid of the laptop.

'What?' she says, like he's not welcome.

Joey turns towards the doorway so she can acknowledge the presence of Rodney.

'I can see him,' she whines, and she goes to open her laptop once more, but Joey places his fingertips there to prevent her. 'I'm trying to watch something.'

But she doesn't persist. She closes the lid completely and pulls the earphones from her ears and lets them flop on the table.

'Where's your ma?'

She lets out a loud groan. 'I don't know where she is.'

'What do you mean?'

'I mean I don't know where she is. She just left and said she won't be back until I'm gone from here.'

'Ah Jesus, Sharon!' Rodney says from the doorway.

Sharon frowns at him like he's a stranger. Joey laughs.

'It's not funny, Joey,' Rodney says.

'The only reason her ma up and left is because she wants Sharon to see sense and get back to Trinity where she belongs.'

'I don't belong there. I never belonged. I belong here. I'll get a job in a shop or I'll volunteer in the local school.'

Rodney takes this as a signal to come across to the table. He pulls out a chair and places it right beside her and leans in his head so she can't ignore him. 'Come on, Sharon, don't say that. You belong in Trinity. You're the smartest person in there.'

'Ah here,' says Joey, 'I wouldn't say that now, Rodney.'

'Fuck you, Joey,' Sharon snaps and her lower lip quivers like she's ready to cry.

Joey reaches across the table and places his hand gently on her fingers. She makes to pull her hand away but doesn't seem to have the energy.

'Where's Weso?' Joey asks.

'He doesn't live here any more,' Sharon says.

'He's moved out?'

'Ma asked him to leave when she heard who he's working for.'

'Your ma is a fucking legend,' Joey says. 'And so are you!'

Sharon sniffs but doesn't argue. It's news to Joey about Weso moving out of the house. He never told Joey that he'd moved or was planning to.

'Look at me, Sharon,' Joey says. And she does. He can see the red blotchy patches beneath both eyes where she's been wiping away tears and mascara. 'What the fuck, Sharon. You've outgrown this place. It's not you any more. It's not.'

'I come from an estate like this too, Sharon,' Rodney chips in.

'Fuck off, Rodney! No way!' Joey can't help but say, and even Sharon's eyes go wide with surprise.

He laughs. 'Yeah, I give my address as Montenotte but it's the estate beside it I'm really from. My ma works as a cleaner in the local school, my da drives a cement lorry, and there's five lads and one girl younger than me, so you can imagine what it was like in a three bed semi-fuckin'-D.'

'But your accent, Rodney?' Joey says.

'Yeah, I know. I used get slagged off in school because of the way I spoke. Posh Head they used call me, as well as other stuff. You know, like, black *and* gay. That wasn't easy to grow up with. But I'm out of there now and I ain't ever going back. And you're the same as me, Sharon.'

'Yeah, Sharon. You and Rodney are out of the same sliced pan. But I'm not. I know that and I'm not going to fuck it up on you. I promise. And you can't let that Ber one do it to you either.'

'You told him what happened?' she says, looking at Rodney, but there's not much of an accusation in it.

He nods.

'And I'm staying away from you, Sharon, until I figure out what's going on with Vinnie.'

'But Miles doesn't like me any more! He wouldn't speak to me even when I wanted to say I was sorry.'

'Miles will get over it,' Rodney chimes in. 'And what you said about Bernice should have been said a long time ago. She can be a bitch. Everyone knows that. You can't let her drive you out.'

'Miles doesn't think she's a bitch.'

'Miles does, but he'd never say it. The two of them have been friends, like, for ever.'

'You hear that, Sharon? Your two lads think she's a bitch. And I had her sussed the first time I set eyes on her.'

'Sure you did, Joey. I needed a mop to clean up the drool any time you were near her.'

Rodney laughs out loud and holds his two hands against his stomach, but it's such a pleasing laugh and so warm it seems to melt some of Sharon's bad mood. She pulls her hand away from Joey's. It's then the doorbell rings and all three of them turn towards the door leading to the hallway. The bell rings again but none of them move.

'Aren't you going to answer it?' Joey asks.

'No! And you're not to either,' Sharon warns.

'What if it's your ma and she's forgotten her key?'

'It's not my ma,' Sharon says, like she can see through walls.

The bell rings once more and then there's the loud rap of knuckles on glass.

'It could be Weso coming back for something?'

'He has a key, and anyway he'd come round the back and try and get in that way.'

The bell rings again and it's getting to be annoying.

'Fuck this!' Joey says and he gets to his feet.

When he opens the door, he sees the back of a guy whose heading towards the gate. The guy stops and turns.

'Mag– eh, Stephen! What the fuck are you doing out this time of night?'

'Very funny, Joey. It's only ten o'clock and I'm freezing out here.

He's wearing only a T-shirt and jeans, but he's got a Spar bag dangling from one hand and Joey can see the shape of the cans that are inside it.

'How did you know we were here?'

Stephen comes back up the path. 'Rodney rang me looking for your number and told me about Sharon doing a runner, so I thought I might come round and cheer her up.'

He lifts the bag like that's where all the cheer is and Joey smiles and stands aside to let him in.

Sharon frowns when she sees him and then looks at Joey and Rodney, as if they've planned the whole thing.

'Who's the most popular girl in Trinity?' Joey says.

'Fuck you, Joey!' Sharon says, but he can sense her mood brightening even more.

'SHARON! SHARON! SHARON!' Joey now chants and the other pair join in.

'Fuck you all!' she cries, but ruins it with the small smile she lets slip.

'Just for you, Sharon,' Stephen says a little shyly as he deposits the bag on the table and pulls out a naggin of gin and a couple of limes. 'I'll go and make it the way you like it.'

'What did you pay for that naggin?' Joey is curious to know, as Stephen heads to the fridge in search of ice.

'It was cheaper than in that kip you work in, Joey,' Stephen says, and Joey takes a can from the bag and hands it to Rodney, who is taking the makings of a joint from his tobacco pouch.

'Excuse me!' Sharon says loudly, like she wants to make an announcement and they all stand still and turn to face her. 'Excuse me, but what is going on here? I come home for some peace and quiet and now I find the three of you here like you're ready to party.'

Stephen laughs and releases ice cubes that tinkle into the glass he's taken down from a shelf above the fridge. Rodney smiles his big catlike smile as he licks the joint together. And Joey pulls the tab on a can like it's a grenade, then sits back and absorbs the explosion in his empty stomach. Sharon looks from one of them to the other but can't find anything else to say. She shakes her head and folds her arms, then peers at the gin and ice and sliver of lime that Stephen has deposited in the glass for her with the small can of tonic water beside it.

'Thanks, Stevie,' she says, and he beams at her and takes a can for himself, then sits at the table.

Rodney lights up and passes the joint around and Stephen coughs and splutters before passing it on and all three of them laugh but say nothing except for Joey.

'Lightweight!'

'Oh my God, that makes up for all those other names,' Stephen says and laughs.

'Don't tell me Joey gave you a hard time?' Rodney says.

'He was a shit,' Stephen and Sharon say in unison, and they all laugh.

'Yeah, I was a shit,' Joey says.

Then Rodney's phone pings and he pulls it close to examine the message.

'Miles wondering where you are?' Sharon says.

'Yeah.' He gets up from the table and goes into the hallway.

The three of them listen as he talks.

'Yeah. I'm still here. She's OK. She'll be back tomorrow.'

'I never said I was going back,' Sharon shouts.

'Yeah, that's her! And Stephen and Joey are here. Yeah! He's here. He came out with me. I don't know what we're doing. We're having a drink with Sharon and then I'll probably head back in.'

'You're staying the night,' Sharon shouts. Joey and Stephen stare at her. 'You can all stay.' She glances at Joey. 'I'm staying in my ma's bedroom. Rodney can sleep in my old room and the pair of yous can fight over Weso's.'

Then Rodney is back in with the phone in his hand.

'Miles wants to talk to you, Sharon,' he says and hands her his phone. Sharon takes it and goes to the hallway to talk.

They listen but this time they can't really hear much of what's being said because her voice is soft. Rodney wants to know more about how Stephen and Joey got on together in school, but Joey doesn't want to say too much except repeat that he was a shit and is grateful that Stephen doesn't want to expose him for the mean bastard he was. Then Sharon is back and sits once more.

Rodney takes out a pack of cards. 'I'll teach you all how to play twenty-fives,' he says.

'Isn't that an old man's game?' Stephen says.

'I know how to play it!' Sharon pipes up, full of enthusiasm. 'My ma taught me and my brother.'

'Can't be difficult if Sharon knows how to play it,' Joey says and he beams a smile at her. He can see from the look in her eyes that she's softened her attitude towards him, but he's glad the other two are present.

Rodney deals four hands of five and turns a card face up on the pile that's left. He tells them how that card decides what's trumps and how a card's value is higher when red but lower when black and if anyone wants to rob the trump at the top of the deck then they have to have the ace of that suit in order to do it. And he tells them how the five of trumps is the best card in the pack and can beat any other and the next most powerful is the jack followed by the ace then the king and queen. They all catch on very quickly and Joey robs the card that's trumps and Stephen makes a joke about him still doing a bit of robbing and they all laugh and the time flies by and Sharon seems to forget all her troubles to do with college, and Joey forgets all about his worries over what's on the laptop he's brought.

Rodney is checking his phone as he plays, and it's obvious he's under pressure to get back into town. But he seems to be enjoying himself too much to comply with whatever Miles is asking him to do. Eventually he just puts the phone into his pocket and puts all his energy into the game. The table is full of empty cans and there's only half a lime left with the segments of the rest swimming in Sharon's glass.

Rodney is the first to yawn and make an excuse about being tired and Sharon brings him upstairs to show him where he's to sleep. And she tells Joey and

Stephen she won't be back down and she'll see them in the morning.

It's then that Joey remembers the laptop. He takes it out of the bag and places it on the table and uses Sharon's adaptor to recharge it. Stephen has his head slumped on his chest. He stirs when he hears the computer waken. He sits up and looks about, like he's trying to remember where he is.

'Where's everyone gone?'

Joey glances at him but then returns his eyes to the screen, which is not showing anything except for folders that are all empty.

'What's with the laptop?' Stephen asks.

Joey isn't sure how much he should tell him. He turns the laptop towards Stephen, then pushes it nearer to him.

'You know more about these than I do, Stephen. Can you find anything on this laptop? Anything at all?'

Stephen comes to life and sits up straight and wide awake. He taps some keys, then pauses as he stares at the screen, then taps again. He shakes his head.

'Nothing! Like, whose laptop is it? It's not one you've –'

'No, Stephen! I'm not doing that kind of stuff any more.'

'Whose is it? And you need to get that crack fixed before it gets worse.'

'It's Vinnie's. Well, not exactly Vinnie's. More like it belonged to that gangster Quinlan.'

'Vinnie?'

'Yeah. He's back in Dublin.'

'To do what?'

'That's the question everyone is asking, especially Quinlan. I thought it might have something to do with this computer.'

'Your stepda's not going to get in with him again, is he?'

'I don't know what he's up to, Stephen. He says he's come back to, like, turn over a new leaf so we can all play happy families. And he says he's going to keep his head down and just work and bother nobody.'

'So, what's the problem?'

'There's a cop on the scene who says Vinnie is back in Dublin to make trouble for Quinlan. He thinks Vinnie took a computer – maybe this one or maybe it was some other one – but anyway, Vinnie took something that he says can help them arrest Quinlan. He thinks Vinnie is going to be trying his hand at blackmail or some shit like that.'

'And that's the laptop he took?'

'It could be. That's one he gave me.'

'He gave it to you?'

'Yeah. He gave it to me! I couldn't believe it! I pretended I needed one for Sharon and I was hoping he'd give it to me, if he thought Sharon needed it for college ...'

'If he gave you the laptop just like that – that's hardly the plan of a blackmailer.'

'I know, and that's what's puzzling. He just gave it to me. He said he couldn't sell it because of the little crack on the screen and he was probably too mean to get it fixed.'

'Well, there doesn't seem to be anything on it, Joey. Nothing I can find. So maybe he's telling the truth?'

'Maybe. But I don't trust Vinnie just as much as I don't trust Quinlan.'

Joey roots down at the bottom of the computer bag and finds three USB sticks. He stares at them then hands them to Stephen.

'Maybe there's stuff on those.'

Stephen inserts them one at a time and searches for files. He shakes his head after each one. Nothing shows up on the screen. Then Joey roots once more in the case. There's nothing else there. But as he withdraws his hand it brushes against a small zip in the side lining. He unzips it. He lets his fingers root inside and he pulls out another USB stick and hands it to Stephen.

Stephen inserts it and taps some keys, then he moves his head back from the screen, like what he sees might contaminate him in some way.

'Fucking hell!' he says.

'What?'

'There's names and numbers here and photos of all sorts of bad shit.'

'What do you mean – bad shit?'

'Look for yourself,' Stephen says and he turns the screen to face Joey.

The first photo Joey sees is of two sinister-looking heavies who are sitting on red seats with plush-looking purple curtains behind them. Each of them has a topless woman on his lap. The women are wearing very little except for black thongs and stiletto heels. One of the men has a gun in his hand and he's holding it like he's James Bond. The other man with his shadow beard has no gun.

But it looks like he's given it to the girl he's with. She's staring at the camera and smiling. The gun is an Uzi. The second photo shows Quinlan on the same red velvet seats and he's lighting a cigar with a fifty-euro note. Quinlan is posing in a lot of the photos after that and they're taken somewhere foreign because of the blue skies and the pool umbrellas like it's his own holiday home he's in. There's a photo of him in a wooded area standing legs apart with a gun aimed at a distant target. In one of the photos he has his arm around a young girl who's fake-smiling, and it's a dodgy-looking photo to say the least.

Joey doesn't recognise anyone in any of the photos, other than Quinlan. Some look foreign, but most have Irish sunburnt heads on them and they're not much older than the scooter heads that have been tailing him.

He drifts the cursor down and scrolls through page after page of the names and figures. A lot of the names are Irish sounding and there's addresses beside them and figures showing thousands of euros. He scrolls down once more and there's another show of photos. He scrolls through them, but then stops suddenly and peers closer to the screen.

'Holy shit!' he cries, then scrolls once more before pulling his fingers away from the keys like they've just been burned.

'Holy fuckin' shit!' he says, and he rubs his hands on his face, then stares at the screen like he needs to be certain.

'What? What is it?' Stephen wants to know, and Joey turns the screen towards him but doesn't let it go because he wants to see what else is there.

'It's that cop I was telling you about. He's there – with Quinlan and his gang or someone else's gang. Look at him. He's got his hands all over that young girl in that photo and what age is she supposed to be? And scroll down through them. He's there and he looks plastered and laughing with all those evil-looking fuckers like he's best mates with them all.'

'So, what's going on?'

'He's bent. That's what's going on. He doesn't want Quinlan brought down. He's trying to save himself! And he wants Quinlan to help him and obviously Quinlan needs him where he is.'

'Fucking hell, Joey! What are you going to do?'

'Fuck!' Joey says and takes the last swallow of beer from his last can. 'Fuck!' he says again.

'So, it might have nothing at all to do with Vinnie,' Stephen says, 'except they're afraid he might have seen all of this and is back to make trouble.'

'Yeah, but if Vinnie knew that was there, he wouldn't have given me the laptop. No way he'd have done that. I don't know what he'd have done with it.'

'So, what are you going to do with this shit?'

'I'm going to make copies of it, Stephen, and give them to …' He pauses and rubs at his mouth with his hand.

'Give them to who?'

'I don't know.'

'I don't want a copy anyway,' Stephen says quickly. 'That's the sort of shit that could get you killed, Joey. That's the sort of shit I see all the time in those stories on the telly. You don't mess with those fuckers, Joey. You don't. They'd cut your head off and post it to your ma.'

'Fucksake, Stephen! You don't have to make it sound that bad.'

'What sounds bad?' Sharon asks in a drunken drawl, coming through the doorway, dressed in pyjama shorts and a white T-shirt.

Joey closes the laptop cover.

'Don't tell me the pair of you are watching porn?' she says, heading to the sink and filling a Guinness pint glass with water from the tap.

'Hey, we're not like that, Sharon,' Stephen says like he's offended.

'Maybe you're not, Stevie,' she says and ruffles his hair as she's passing back towards the door.

Stephen's face turns beetroot and he rubs his cheeks to try and conceal the colour. Now Sharon has her hand on Joey's shoulder.

'Can I talk to you?' she says. He turns to look at her and she indicates with an upward turn of her eyes that she wants him upstairs.

'Mind that laptop for me, *Stevie*,' he says. 'I'll be back down in a jiff.'

Sharon's ma's room is neat and clean. There's a comfortable armchair beside a double bed with a lighted lamp and a clock radio on a bedside locker. There's a bookshelf with books near the window and the room has one wall papered and there's a print of Marilyn Monroe on it. He knows it's Marilyn Monroe because Sharon showed him a photo of the picture when she bought it for her ma. There's a photo on the bookshelf of Sharon and her da. She's only four in it and it was the week before he died of an overdose. Sharon moves her phone out of her way so she can climb back into her side of the bed.

Joey stands there looking at her. 'I thought you wanted nothing more to do with me.'

'I don't but I … I just need you to stay here until I fall asleep,' she says.

He moves to lie beside her on the bed but she points to the armchair. 'Sit there, Joey.'

He sits and untangles a knot on one of his runners.

'I need to get a job, Joey.'

'Yeah?'

'Yeah. I'm running out of money – the money I saved during the summer. The grant isn't going to cover everything, and I don't want to be asking Ma, or have to come back and live here.'

'Yeah, I can imagine.'

'You could put in a word for me, Joey.'

'Where?'

'With Hazel.'

'Yeah, sure!'

'Are you listening to me, Joey?'

'Yeah. You want a job.'

He pulls off both runners and watches her now as she stares up at the ceiling.

'What's going to happen to us?' she asks.

'Who?'

'Me! You! My stupid brother. My ma. What's going to happen to us? Like, what am I even doing? I don't know what I'm doing. I'm making a fool of myself.'

Joey doesn't know what to say because he feels the same way himself. What's he to do with all those photos? He can't show them to Vinnie in case he might want to use them to blackmail the cop, or Quinlan. That would be something Vinnie might well do. He might think it's a far easier way to get money than selling dodgy boxes. And he's worried for Stephen because now he's shown him the contents of the USB stick. That was a mistake. He can't involve Stephen in his shit like he involved Sharon. He knows he has to stay away from Sharon until he decides what to do next. But it feels like tonight he's doing some good, like getting her back to college and now sitting there watching over her like a guardian angel.

He snuggles into the armchair and lets his head rest against the back of it. He closes his eyes and sees the photo of Quinlan with his arm snaked around that young girl who doesn't look much older than Isabel. He opens his eyes and watches Sharon as she turns away from him and sighs into her pillow. His eyelids are heavy and he lets them close once more, knowing other images besides those of Quinlan and Doyle will flash before him. He's going to see his da on the floor of that bookshop and Amber's da on the footpath. He's so tired he doesn't care who shows up. Maybe he knows, like for the first time, how impossible it is not to see something when his camera eyes have lodged all the photos in his brain.

He wakes with a start when he hears the front door open. He glances at the clock radio and sees he's been asleep for over an hour and a half. He thinks that Stephen is heading home because he's not too far away from his gaff. But it's not Stephen leaving. It's someone else, because he hears Stephen come back into the kitchen. It must be Rodney, maybe, who has had a change of mind, but he doesn't like the thought of him wandering round on his own at this time of night. He goes quietly down the stairs to check it out. Stephen is tidying away the cans and there's two mugs on the table and an open Brennan's batch loaf and the smell of toast.

'Who was here?' Joey asks.

Stephen turns round from where he's standing by the sink. 'It was just one of the lads from college looking for a bit of company.'

'Company?'

'Well, to be honest, I'd … I'd borrowed money off him, and he was looking for it back.'

'And you were able to give it to him?'

'Yeah.'

Joey sees the laptop on the table with the USB attached to its side.

'You didn't …?'

'No way!' Stephen turns back to the sink and rinses out Sharon's glass and leaves it upside down to drain on the worktop. 'I made him tea and toast and then he said he had somewhere else to be. That was it.'

Stephen says he'll sleep on the couch in the sitting room, but Joey tells him to go upstairs and sleep in Weso's old room. Stephen hesitates, like he's afraid Weso might arrive in and murder him. But he goes, and Joey sits at the table and peers once more at the laptop. He should be feeling sleepy now, but he's wide awake.

24

'Well?' is all that Vinnie's text to him says.

He stares at the word for an age, then replies:

Sharon loves the laptop.
She said thanks.

Vinnie doesn't reply and Joey is relieved. He's not sure if he was right to give him his number, but maybe everything will be different now because – maybe Vinnie is telling him the truth. Maybe! His head is full of maybes.

He makes his way from work, his mind racing. When he gets near the gate that leads to the short-cut, Joey notices the boy leaning against the bonnet of a navy VW. He's wearing a black tracksuit and his runners are off-the-shelf-white. His hoodie is up with his earphones plugged in and his head bouncing. The boy doesn't see him but he's right next to the gate, like he's watching for him. His scooter is on the path just beyond the boot of the car. There's an empty parking space there and Joey sees the van that's reversing now to take up the spot. Joey nudges the scooter with his elbow and it topples sideways onto the roadway, and as he walks on, he can hear the crunching sound of steel not wanting to bend. The boy is suddenly alert, and scurries to the roadside to shout abuse at the van driver. Joey calmly enters the short passageway, and as the gate bangs shut behind him it's the first time he's smiled all day.

Once inside Jackie's door he can hear voices. Jackie has a caller and he's sure it will be Martin. There's no smell of a scented candle, though, so it might not be him. He doesn't really care because he'll go to his room.

It's not Martin. It's Doyle.

'Ah, here he is now,' Jackie says, sounding relieved like her head's been done in making small talk.

Joey stares at the cop. His clothes are different now. He's wearing a long-sleeved black T-shirt beneath a black sleeveless puffer jacket. His jeans are blue and faded, but he has the same pair of expensive runners on his feet. He's sitting back in the armchair with his legs crossed, all comfortable like, but sits up and leans forward as soon as Joey enters the room.

Joey stands there and stares at the guy, then looks towards Jackie like he's due an explanation.

'He's just wondering if you heard from Vinnie? I've already told him I haven't, and we really don't want anything more to do with him.'

'I spoke to him,' Joey says.

'You did?' Jackie and the cop say together.

'When? Where?' Jackie asks.

The cop is cooler about it, though Joey can see from the way his eyes light up that he's more than interested.

'He rang me!'

'And?' Jackie asks.

'And really nothing.' He looks at Doyle. 'I told him what you told me about Quinlan – how he's thinking Vinnie's come back here to make trouble – and how you want to bring Quinlan down by using whatever it is Vinnie is supposed to have on him.'

'And what did he say to that?' Doyle asks, keeping his voice calm, but his eyes have gone all anxious on him.

Joey looks towards Jackie, but her eyes aren't signalling anything in particular.

'He just said he's back here because this is his home. He wants to be near where his family live. He's keeping his head down and just working long hours.'

'At what?' Doyle asks.

'I dunno. He didn't say, but I presume it's something to do with cars.'

'And no other mention of Quinlan?'

'No! And when I told him what you said, he just laughed. The only thing he took from Quinlan was the car and a laptop. The car he said was a banger.' He's not going to tell them Vinnie sold it.

'And the laptop?'

'Vinnie said he couldn't use it because he forgot it was in the boot of the car and then threw a wheel in on top of it and cracked the screen. He made shite of it. He said he didn't bother to get it fixed because the money they were asking for was crazy. And anyway, he said, he hates computers, prefers the pen and paper.'

'And that was it?'

'Yeah … well, he told me I could have the laptop if I wanted to spend money on a new screen.'

'He said *you* could have it?' Doyle looks like he's trying his best not to spring up out of the armchair.

Jackie is watchful and silent, leaving the questioning to the expert.

'Yeah, I actually have it. A courier dropped it into the shop.'

'You actually have it … *here?*'

'Oh my God, Joey, I think you should hand it over now,' Jackie suggests.

The cop sits back in his seat like there's nothing to get excited about.

'You don't need to be spending money on a new screen, Joey,' Jackie says. 'Isn't the laptop I gave you good enough – for all you ever do on it?'

'Yeah. I know. I just took it, like, to please him … and also, I suppose … just in case it has something that Detective Doyle here could use.' Joey turns to Doyle now. 'Like, you're not the only one who wants to see Quinlan put away. He's a scumbag!'

'Joey! Please don't use that word. It's not nice.'

Doyle turns to smile at Jackie. 'It's OK. I've heard him called a lot worse.'

He places his hands on his knees and exhales as if with relief.

'Go and get the laptop for him, Joey, so we can all relax about Vinnie.'

'Are you sure you'll be able to use it?' Joey says. 'I mean, the screen is totally fucked.'

'Joey!'

'Cracked! It's totally fuckin' cracked.'

Jackie groans. 'Will you just go and get it! Detective Doyle has people who can get beyond cracked screens. Or at least they'll find the money to put on a new one.'

'Oh, I'm not sure about that now.' Doyle laughs. 'Money's always tight in my line of business.'

Joey sniffs. *What exactly is your business?* He'd like to ask him this, but stays silent, just heads for his bedroom. He stops in his tracks when Doyle calls his name. The cop is leaning forward once more in his seat.

'And was there a ... a case with it?'

'Yeah. You want that as well?'

'Yeah, why not?'

Joey notices the change that's come over the cop's features. There's a sort of hopeful eagerness in his eyes along with the anxiety.

He hears a bit of small talk between them about the weather, but when he comes back into the room the cop is on his feet and immediately takes hold of the computer bag. He brings it across to the island table and unzips it. He has his back to them now, but Joey knows what he's searching for. He sees him take the laptop out of the case and place it to one side. Then he dips into the case once more and Joey can see the tiny movement his hand makes as his fingers go searching. Then he sees him freeze as the fingers find the USB that's hidden there. Joey watches him extract it and slip it into his inside jacket pocket, then turn to the pair of them.

'I've a strong feeling this could all be one huge misunderstanding. I'll get this laptop checked out with the IT lads. And – and if there's nothing on it – and Vinnie continues to keep his head down then maybe I'll – we'll have to find some other way to take Quinlan down.'

He puts the laptop back in the bag and zips it up.

'I'll get this back to you – if there's nothing incriminating on it.'

'I don't want it back. You can keep it.'

'Are you sure? Because I can drop it off to your workplace.'

'Naw, it's OK. Anyway, I don't work there any more.'

'What?' Jackie says, shocked.

'I forgot to tell you, Jackie. I quit my job today. I'm going working somewhere else.'

Doyle has lost interest now in the pair of them and is trying not to show he's in a hurry out the door.

'I'm going into the restaurant business,' Joey says.

25

Joey can't understand a word that's being spoken in the kitchen. Luca's hands are going as fast as his mouth, and Matteo – Tina's da – is either agreeing with him, or else he's shaking his head like Luca is talking shite. And it could be shite, but any time Joey hears someone speak a foreign language he always thinks they must be very clever to have mastered something that seems so alien to him. Luca has fuck all English and is in college in Italy, but has taken a year out to come and learn English in the café. Tina has told Joey that her father Matteo will speak only Italian to him, but Luca is to speak only English. He's coming to the end of his shift and already Joey's head is done in with 'Jo-ee! How you say this in ingelish? How you say that?'

Luca is Tina's first cousin and is twenty-one, though he looks about twelve, with his head of curls and his open smile and eyes that seem to love everything they behold. He and Matteo have been talking like motormouths all day, and they might even be talking about him at times, but he hasn't a clue. Every now and then he hears Tina's name and he looks at them and they laugh. And then Luca says the name and Joey turns to look at him and sees him turn away and smile and he knows now it's a game Luca is playing, so the next time he hears her name he just keeps his head down.

He has loaded the dishwasher the way they want it stacked, but can't remember which of the cycles he should run it on. So he just presses the start button and hears the water spilling and leaves well enough alone and hopes for the best.

Luca has shown him all the wooden items that can't be put in the dishwasher and he must do by hand. And he has to be extra careful with the wine glasses cos every one that breaks will come out of his pay. It's amazing how easy he can understand sign language and 'denaro' is the first of his words he's already learned along with 'grassy' and 'chow'.

'Spondulicks', Joey tells him, is the correct word for money in Dublin, and he can only laugh as he hears the poor lad repeat it like a parrot to Tina's ma, Detta. Tina, he now knows, is short for Valentina. He's surprised Sharon didn't tell him that and he should have copped she was Italian when he first met her. But he has taken an instant liking to them all, especially Luca, and he just hopes that he doesn't mess up and make Tina look bad for offering him the job.

Luca hands him a mop, and Joey is busy out front using it when Tina arrives in from college. 'Bon jurno!' he says to her and she beams a smile at him.

Then he hears the explosion of greetings coming from inside as they welcome her home. He keeps mopping until she comes back out with a plateful of pizza slices and two glasses of red wine.

She places them on the table nearest Joey and sits. 'So how did your first day go?'

'Do they ever stop talking?' Joey says.

She laughs and takes a sip of wine, before lifting up two slices and delicately separating them like they've been glued together.

'Join me, will yeh?' she says in her Dub accent, and he glances up at the big old-fashioned brown clock on the wall.

'I've still got half an hour to go,' he says.

'I'll finish up for you. Come on.'

Joey doesn't need to be asked a second time.

'That apron suits you,' she says to him.

He glances down at the front of it and there is a stain from a dollop of tomato sauce on it. He doesn't know if he's supposed to wash it himself and doesn't want to ask in case he has to.

'Yeah, it's grand, especially the faux-leather straps. Are you sure yer one Bernice didn't design it?'

'I wouldn't have anything she designed anywhere near here. Maybe if she made snot-rags I'd use them.'

Joey chuckles and takes a bite from the pizza slice.

'These are a-fuckin-mazing,' he says, and now he gulps down a sip of wine though he'd rather it was beer. He could take a bottle from the fridge but he doesn't want to create any wrong impression.

'I'll teach you how to make pizza base,' she says.

'Yeah?'

'Yeah. And I'll show you how to make proper coffee and use the till so you won't always have to be slaving in the kitchen.'

'Deadly!' Joey says and he's delighted to know that he'll be learning useful stuff that he can put on a CV. That's what Sharon says he needs to be able to do.

'You going to tell Sharon I'm working here?'

She shrugs. 'Maybe. If your name comes up – but I don't know. She seems to have cooled on you – and she's not overly fond of me.'

Joey doesn't say anything, just starts on another slice of pizza. Then the door to the kitchen swings open, and Luca is there with a bottle of beer in his hand.

'Hey, Tina, what's the crack?'

Tina smiles and shakes her head.

'I'm good, Luca. How you doing?'

'I'm working me bollix off,' he says. Then he hears his name called from behind him and he turns and disappears.

'For fucksake, Joey! No!'

'What?'

'You know what!' She gives him a hard stare.

Joey laughs out loud. 'OK, OK, I won't teach him nothing!'

Tina can't even reply to that, because Luca is back out and pulls up a chair to sit beside them. Italian words gush from his mouth and his hands are all over the gaff like he's leading an orchestra of thousands. Tina fires Italian words back at him.

Then Luca is summoned once more from inside the kitchen and he groans like he's the bold child in the family and disappears in a sulk back inside.

'What was he saying?'

Tina shakes her head, but he can see the smile on the corners of her lips that are lovelier now with the wetness of wine on them.

'What?' he asks again.

'He said that we would make beautiful children.'

Joey smiles and catches her eyes and her shyness.

26

Joey is on his way home and cutting round Busáras when the car pulls in beside him, just like it did when this whole Vinnie business kicked off. The passenger window slides open and it's Quinlan's baldy head he sees, though the tan colour has faded like he's forgetting to polish it.

He sees Weso at the wheel and he's back to ignoring him once more. He can understand why. It's the fucker in the back seat that makes Joey pull his head back and away from the car. Ginsey McGinn is sitting in there.

'Get in,' Quinlan orders, and Joey feels like walking on, but hesitates. It's best to get this sorted once and for all, so everyone can get on with their lives.

'I'm tired,' Joey says. 'I'm on my way home.'

'Get the fuck in!' Quinlan snaps and Joey bends down to look through the rear door window to make sure the Ginsey fucker has moved over.

Hopefully Quinlan is going to tell him that everything is OK now because Doyle has passed on the news about their operation being safe. And Joey would like to tell Quinlan that he's seen the photos and knows all about the crooked cop, but he's not stupid enough to make that mistake. And now that the bad feeling with Vinnie is sorted, maybe Quinlan is trying to patch things up between himself and Ginsey. But maybe that's being a bit too hopeful – as if Quinlan wants to be a social worker!

Joey sits in, and Ginsey is acting like Joey isn't even there. And he hasn't got his crutch with him. It could be he's completely cured of his limp or else he doesn't want to appear weak in front of Quinlan.

Joey waits for Quinlan to say something.

'Drive!' is what he does say, and Weso puts the car in motion and they head out the coast road towards Fairview.

Joey doesn't know what's going on. He'd like to take his phone out and text Jackie to let her know he's not sure when he'll be back. But he thinks better of doing that. Like, why worry her when he doesn't even know himself if he should be worried?

They go past the turn-off for Amber's school and the church that's down the road from it where he met her ma and her priest guy. There are cyclists aplenty on the cycle track on his right and the water looks choppy and cold, reflecting the grey of the sky.

Weso takes a right turn off the main road and now it looks like they're heading out towards Dollymount strand. He kinda remembers it from a visit he made with his ma when they did that sort of stuff and Dublin hadn't shrunk to just his estate.

They drive down the wide finger of road that's between like two lakes of water as if they're heading across to the island and he can see the grassy sand dunes in the distance and there's loads of car-parking places on his left.

Weso pulls the car into a space that has no other cars within fifty metres of it. As soon as they stop, Joey hears Quinlan's front window slide down and Quinlan now has a pair of binoculars in his hands and he's adjusting them in front of his eyes like he's one of the minions from *Despicable Me*.

'Fuckin' shelducks! I love them birds,' he says.

Joey can't imagine Quinlan being into birdwatching, but maybe the guy has a side he doesn't know about, like maybe he's got a massive stamp collection at home. Though Quinlan's 'stamp' collection more than likely is a collection of boots. Joey smiles at the idea. A seagull glides away over the water and then there's a swarm of other birds that he knows are some sort of duck. Maybe Quinlan might tell them what these are called, like he's yer man Attenborough off the telly.

They're all silent now and Joey wishes Weso would say something so he doesn't feel like he's out here on his own.

Then Joey sees Quinlan's hand between the seats and he's holding a large brown envelope in it. Joey stares at it, then realises he's supposed to take it. He does take it.

'Open it!' Quinlan hisses and the front window slides shut.

Joey opens the flap and peers inside the envelope, like just in case Quinlan's put a rat trap in it that might snap his fingers off. He pulls out four large photographs. He can feel Weso's eyes on him, and when he looks at the mirror, he sees him glance away towards the sea.

Joey has to suppress a small gasp of surprise. He has seen two of these photos already. One is of Quinlan with the fifty-euro note and one is of the scary dudes with their guns and gangster molls on their laps. He doesn't need to look at the other two photos to know that this means trouble. He stuffs all four back into the envelope and places them on the ledge that's between the front seats.

'You getting into the movie business or what?' Joey says, trying to keep it light; but he knows it's the wrong thing to say. He can hear Ginsey make a sniff like he enjoyed the joke but he can also see Weso turn his head to gauge Quinlan's reaction.

Quinlan's face is stone as he takes back the envelope, then gets out of the car. All three lads watch him as he pulls a cigarette from a packet and lights up.

'What the fuck?' Joey says in the direction of Weso's head.

But Weso ignores him as if his boss is still in the car.

Joey's door opens and he knows it's an invitation to get out. He wants to say something to Weso. He wants to ask him again what's going on, but he knows now isn't the time.

Joey steps out of the car, and Quinlan turns round to face him.

'I don't get it,' Joey says. 'Like, what do I need to look at your photos for? I mean, everyone can go on holidays wherever they please and with whoever they want. What's the big deal? Like, why did you bring me out here?'

Quinlan throws his smoke away and takes a step closer to Joey so he's in Joey's face.

'Those photos were sent to me by Vinnie. He says he's got fifty or so of them and a list of names and numbers. He says I wouldn't like it if they got out. My wife wouldn't like it. My kids wouldn't like it. And I'd probably have the cops on my back and wanting to take everything I have away from me.'

'You were talking to him?'

'No! I wasn't talking to him. The envelope was dropped off at the garage.'

'And he wrote all that? What you said?'

'Typed. He didn't write it because he knows not to do something stupid like that.'

'So how do you know it was Vinnie?'

'Because of the 'V' at the end.'

'And what does he want?'

'He wants a hundred grand – cash. He didn't give the details yet but he said he'll be doing that soon.'

Joey falls silent while Quinlan takes out another smoke and lights it up. He takes two pulls and then holds it down by his side as he surveys the new group of birds that have flown in and have landed on the water.

'That's not going to happen,' Quinlan says.

'What's not going to happen?'

'Vinnie getting my money. Not gonna happen.'

Joey wants to say this has nothing to do with him. He just wants to get home and put his tired feet up and watch the telly or chat to Jackie if she's home. But what's going on? What's Vinnie at? Did he find all the stuff on the laptop and copy it and then clean it off but didn't see the USB stick? Does he know about the crooked cop? This is typical Vinnie – trying to make easy money once again. And once again he's dragged Joey into it.

Quinlan gets back into the car and Joey waits until he's seated before he goes to the car door to open it and get in. He needs time to think. He presses the handle of the door but it won't open. He tries it a second time but it won't budge.

Quinlan's window slides down and he starts talking to Joey from inside the car.

'Ginsey here told me about that incident out near your Luas stop. He thought the man on the motorbike had something to do with me ... but I've assured him I know nothing about it and now he's thinking ... and I'm thinking ...'

'It wasn't Vinnie. It was just some local guy who didn't want to see me getting hurt.'

'Sure, but me and Ginsey here are convinced otherwise.'

'It wasn't Vinnie,' Joey says, but he knows they don't believe him.

'You've been slow to get the message, Joey. I thought you were clever, but maybe I've been wrong about that. I'll say it one more time so it's clear. Me and your stepda need to have a chat in order for him to understand he can't continue to live here if he's trying to blackmail me. And I know he might want to be in the same city as his family, but – and I don't like saying this to you, Joey, because I'm quite fond of you – he's putting every one of you at risk by pulling this kind of stunt. Ginsey here is just champing at the bit to be let loose.' Then the window slides up, and Weso pulls out without indicating, and Joey watches the car as it fades in the distance before turning left towards town.

27

When he gets to Jackie's, he hears voices coming from the kitchen. Maybe she's brought Off-Licence Martin home once more. But it's not Martin he meets but his ma.

She stands up and comes quickly towards him and wraps him in a hug.

'Where were you until this time?' Jackie says like she's the ma now. 'I've kept dinner for you.'

'Got delayed. Had to do a bit of extra cleaning up.'

'Oh my God, Joey, Jackie told me all about your new job. It's so exciting.'

'Yeah, Ma! Scrubbing dishes and mopping floors.'

'Hey, welcome to our world,' Jackie says and she and his ma have a good laugh at that. He goes to the cooker.

'It's in the microwave,' Jackie says. 'Your ma brought us some pizza and I made a nice salad to go with it.

Joey heats the pizza, though he's had enough of it for one day, but doesn't say that because he doesn't want to sound ungrateful.

When he sits to eat it, he can see both of them watching him like they're expecting him to make some sort of announcement, or they think it's the best pizza ever and they're awaiting his opinion. He wants to tell them about all that's happened. He wants their advice. Isn't that what a ma and an aunt are there for? What the fuck is he to do now with all the info that's bouncing in his brain?

'What?' he says like their stares are bugging him.

'It's about Vinnie.'

'Has something happened?'

How could something have happened? It's too soon and Quinlan and Doyle don't know where he's living.

'No, Joey,' his ma says. 'It's just me and Jackie have been talking and we thought maybe it's time for us to let him come back into the family – to let him know we're here for him.' She turns then to Jackie. 'Tell Joey what happened last night.'

Joey stares at his aunt.

'I was at choir practice. With Martin. We were all there and there was this man down at the back of the church listening to us. He was dressed in bike leathers and he'd the helmet on his lap and he looked like he'd come in for a rest or ... I dunno ... I thought he knew one of the women in the group and he'd come to support her. His hair was so long and a beard like Jesus has in the stations of the cross that are on the church walls out there. He was just sitting there and I could see he was making Martin a bit nervous.

'It was Vinnie, Joey,' his ma cries, like Jackie is taking too long as usual to tell her story.

'Vinnie?'

'Yes,' Jackie says and shakes her head.

'But tell him the rest of it,' his ma urges her.

'Martin asked us if any of us knew him and nobody did, so he went and asked him was he OK and he said he was just in to listen and Martin was delighted because he thought he might be interested in joining at some stage. And he just sat there while we sang and there was something sad about him – something in the way he was sitting with hunched shoulders that was telling me about his loneliness. I kept watching him and I could see him watching me also. It was the strangest thing ever. He stayed there until near the end, with his head bowed, just listening to the choir. I knew he knew I was watching him … and it felt … it felt to me like he just wanted to be there because I was there. Like he could be back with us again.' There are tears welling up in her eyes and her voice falters. She takes another sip, then sighs.

'Oh, for fucksake!' Joey shouts and he covers his eyes with his hands.

'What?' his ma and Jackie cry out together. He lowers his hands and stares in bewilderment at them both.

'Are yous stupid? Yiz want to take him back? Will yiz ever learn? That was just a stunt he pulled. A stunt! For sympathy. He doesn't care about you, Ma, and he doesn't care about you either, Jackie. And he doesn't give a shit about Isabel and he definitely doesn't give a shit about me. All he cares about is himself.'

And with that Joey gets up suddenly and heads out the door.

28

He has to find Magpie. Stephen. He has to find Stephen and talk to him. Stephen is the only one who might be able to give Joey advice about what to do. He's the only other person who knows about Quinlan and his bent cop.

But what's Vinnie up to? It doesn't make sense. Unless it's not Vinnie. Maybe it's Doyle that's doing the blackmail. But that doesn't make sense either. Doyle is in a lot of those photos and Quinlan knows too much about what he's been up to. Then Joey remembers the night in Sharon's and Stephen saying he had to pay money back to the guy who came calling. Could he be in trouble with some money lender? Does he need extra funds to keep him in college? Maybe that's why he's sent the photos to Quinlan? But that's not like him. Stephen is afraid of his shadow, or he was anyway. But maybe he's desperate now and Joey has given him the opportunity to get the money he needs. He has to talk to Stephen.

He remembers the house where he brought him home, and he remembers the lads there giving him abuse because of Stephen puking in the kitchen.

Now he's banging on the door because the bell's not working and it's a lad in some sort of GAA jersey made from the Irish flag that opens it.

'What do yeh want?' the lad asks him and Joey knows he's not welcome.

'Is Stephen there?'

The lad turns away and shouts out, 'Hey, Caesar!'

Joey steps inside and leans in close to the lad's face like he's impersonating Quinlan.

'His name's Stephen! OK? So, you'd better call him that.'

The lad's mouth falls open and he takes a backward step and calls out Stephen's name. A door opens behind him and he sees Stephen's head frowning at him.

'It's all right, Matt,' Stephen says, and Matt scurries away into the room that Stephen has just come out of.

'Come on into the kitchen,' Stephen tells him and turns to head in that direction.

Joey follows and Stephen fills a kettle with water and turns it on to boil.

'I don't want anything,' Joey says.

'I do.'

Stephen gets a mug down from the press and throws a tea bag into it that he has taken from a box on a shelf above the kettle. The kitchen is in a state. There's a full black bin bag near the back door that's fallen over and has puked out bits of a broken bowl and a couple of bean cans that still have beans dribbling on the lids. The kitchen floor has some sort of cheap lino on it and it could do with a mop. Then he sees the mop in a corner and gunge clinging to it like someone's used it as a brush. Lads! Their mas must do everything for them. There's nothing on the wooden table except for a selection of crumbs and mug prints and some textbook that can't be too important if a lad left it lying there.

Joey waits to hear what Stephen has to say. But he doesn't seem to be in a hurry to talk. He stands with his back to Joey, his shoulders tense, and pours the boiling water onto his tea bag. Then he brings the mug across to the table where Joey has found the courage to sit. He keeps his hands well clear of the table top.

'Table could do with a wipe,' Joey says.

'They're messy bastards,' Stephen says, 'but I'm not going to be here much longer.'

'Where you going?'

'I don't know, but I'm not staying here.'

'You going home?'

'No! I might go back to my gran's but she doesn't like me bringing anyone in so I don't know. I'll try and get extra hours in the bar and see how it goes then.'

He walks to the black bin bag and pulls it upright and dumps the tea bag into it. He lifts up the cans and places them in the bag, then sweeps the broken shards of bowl with his foot towards the mop like it's some sort of rubbish magnet. He gets a carton of milk from the fridge and pours milk into his tea.

'You sure you don't want anything?'

Joey gives him a definite shake of the head.

'So, Stephen! Is there ... like ... anything you need to tell me?'

Stephen is sitting across from him. Joey stares at him. Stephen lets out a long sigh and wipes the side of his forehead with his fingers.

'I know! I know I should've called you and told you ... but ...'

'What?'

'The other night at Sharon's.'

Joey leans forward to stare at him to let him know he's all ears. 'What about it?'

'It just happened, Joey. I'm sorry!'

'What just happened?

'I went in to check on Sharon in the morning. You and Miles were gone and I told her I'd wait for her and go back into college with her.'

'And?'

'Well, Sharon was kinda crying quietly when I went in, so I sat on the armchair just to keep her company. I said nothing at all. I just said to take her time and sleep on if she needed to. And she fell asleep and I must have dozed off too. But then I hear her calling me and when I open my eyes, she asks me to come lie on the bed beside her.'

'*What*?'

'Yeah.'

'And what did you do?'

'I didn't want to be mean, so ... I just went and lay beside her ... and then she asked me ... like ... to hold her.'

Stephen leans back into his chair like he's expecting a fist to visit his face.

'Nothing happened, Joey! I swear!' He raises his hands in front of his chest like it's a sign of innocence or maybe it's to protect himself.

'Fucksake, Stephen, it's OK!'

'It is? I thought Sharon might have said something about me trying something on with her, and you were here to –'

'For fucksake, Stevie. It's obvious she likes you. And you like her. Anyways you heard her yourself. Me and Sharon are finished. And I don't blame her cos I was just dragging her down. We'll still be mates though. I hope ... but that's not even why I'm here now.'

'Oh!'

'Yeah.'

Stephen sighs loudly. 'That caller?'

'Yeah? Like, who was it?'

'Sorry, Joey, but it wasn't one of the lads from college looking for money.'

'So who was it?'

'It was Weso.'

'WESO!'

'Yeah. He was looking to borrow money off his ma – but he didn't know Sharon was back or that I was there with her. He frightened the shite out of me. I don't know what he thought when he saw me. For a couple of seconds, I thought he didn't even recognise me. He was a bit scary looking. And edgy, like he was on something. You know the way he gets – his eyes get – like he's gone off somewhere. He was going to go up and ask his ma for money, but I told him she wasn't there, that it was Sharon was up in her room. And I told him you were there with her and Rodney was up in his bedroom. And that kinda made him thick. He didn't like the idea of you and Sharon in his ma's room and someone in his bed – like he was one of the three fuckin' bears just come home from walking in the woods – and me in his kitchen with a pile of empty cans.' Stephen pauses and takes in a deep breath.

'Go on!' Joey says.

'I was a bit scared, to tell you the truth because … you know, like … my past history with him. Like I wanted to say, "What the fuck, Weso' – as if he ever gave a shite about any of his family, especially his ma. But I had a twenty and I said he could have it and that kinda calmed him and I made him a gin and tonic and there was a bit of smoke left and that kinda chilled him. But you could see him eyeing the ceiling like he wanted to go up and cause trouble with someone. And then he saw the computer.'

'Aw fuck! No!'

'Yeah. I told him it was yours, that you'd just got it.'

'Aw NO!'

'Sorry, Joey, but he wanted to see what was on it. For a thick fucker he knows his way around computers.'

'Aw no, Stephen, you didn't let him see the photos.'

'I couldn't stop him, especially when he thought I was trying to hide something.'

'He saw them all?'

'Yeah. You should have seen his eyes light up. And he took a copy of them all on one of the USB sticks and he fucked off as soon as he'd that done like not caring a fuck who was eating his porridge or who was up in his ma's bed or his own.'

'Jesus, Stephen, you should have told me. Do you know what he's after doing?'

'No!'

'He's sent photos to Quinlan, pretending they're coming from Vinnie. He's looking for a hundred grand or he's promising to give them to the cops or put them online so Quinlan will be ruined and his crooked cop will be outed.'

Stephen's hands go to hide his face and eyes like he's trying not to see what has happened or the part he's played in it. Then he slides them off.

'For fucksake, Joey! I didn't think he was that stupid.'

'Yeah, exactly what I said.'

'What are you gonna do?'

'I dunno.'

Stephen rubs his hands through his hair and then his chin where there's the shadow of a beard appearing. 'You need to talk to him!' he says.

'It's too late for that,' Joey says.

'Why?'

'Because he's fucked everything up.'

'How?'

'I gave the computer bag to the cop with the computer in it. And I left the USB stick in it, like I'd never found it in the first place. And I could see him discovering it and tucking it away in his pocket, and he looked so relieved – like he was no longer in danger. And I hoped he'd say that to Quinlan so Vinnie would no longer be a problem. He never was a problem anyway, Stephen. He really has come back here for the reason he said, because he wants to be near us all.'

'Fuck!' Stephen says.

'Yeah. But Quinlan says he won't pay the money – so that means they'll want to get Vinnie and silence him for good.'

'But why not just tell Quinlan that it's Weso who sent him the photos, it's Weso who is trying to blackmail him?'

'If I do that, they'll kill Weso, and then I'll have his blood on my hands. And I've enough –' He stops himself from finishing the sentence, then sighs loudly, like he's in despair. 'How could I ever look at Sharon again if I caused anything bad to happen to her brother?'

'You need to go and see Vinnie. You need to tell him everything and see what he can do.'

'But what if he does something mad, like going after Weso? Or worse still, he might think it would be a great idea to go halves with Weso on his plan. He's not beyond doing something crazy like that.'

'Yeah, and if he does that, Joey, you'll know he hasn't changed. You'll know that much. But you have to tell him. You have to.'

'OK. OK, I will.'

'That's good, Joey, because you have to do something. You can't let it drift.'

'OK.' Joey gets up from his chair.

'You're going there now? To talk to Vinnie?'

'Yeah. It's good advice, Stephen. And it was … like … good that you were there for Sharon. Maybe it might have worked out better between us if I was in college, instead of working in Tina's café.'

'You're working in Tina's café?'

'Yeah. What's wrong with that?'

Stephen laughs. 'Of all the cafés, Joey, you'd have to pick that one.'

29

Tina's not impressed when Joey tells her he might be late for work because he has something important to do. And she's not pleased either when he won't tell her what it is that's more important than not screwing up his new career. But he can't tell her anything. He has to get out to Vinnie's place fast and tell him everything like Stephen suggested.

There's no sign of the two scooter heads but he's not taking any chances and follows the same routine as the last time. He heads out on the green Luas a few stops, and he's all eyes alert and as careful as yer man Jason Bourne. So he's sure, by the time he's on the Luas again, back towards the northside, he hasn't been followed.

The steel doors are open, and there are a few bikes out front like before, but there's no sign of either of the men. He can hear Johnny Cash singing about falling into his ring of fire. It's a song his ma likes.

When he's inside he sees one of the men crouching by the side of a bike and doing something to a chain, as he sings along to the song. It's the guy with sleeveless grey overalls. The man seems in a world of his own, so Joey moves quickly to the stairs and climbs them two at a time. He taps on the door and opens it, not waiting for an invitation.

When he's inside, he gets a strong whiff of weed and sees Vinnie and his mate looking up from some sort of document they've been studying at Vinnie's office desk. The man with Vinnie is the grizzly bearded guy. He's got oil on his hands and is keeping them away from whatever they're examining. He's got his long curly hair tied back in a ponytail and he's wearing a red lumberjack shirt this time and a pair of boots that his jeans are stuffed into.

'Joey!' Vinnie sings out, like he's delighted to see him.

The other man says he'll get back down to the ring of fire.

Joey goes to the leather couch and sits. He's not sure how to begin, or how much to tell Vinnie. He might just make things worse than they already are. And he's not sure if he should say anything about Vinnie turning up to watch Jackie at her choir. That was a real Vinnie stunt. So, Joey isn't going to say anything to upset him any more than is necessary.

'Just give me a sec,' Vinnie says, staring down at his document with a pencil in his hand that's hovering over figures.

'I just want to talk to you about that laptop you gave me.'

Vinnie scratches at something on the page and then assesses the change he's made.

'Not enough bells and whistles on it for Sharon?' he says, still intent on his calculations.

'I didn't give it to her.'

'Why not? Keeping it for yourself, are yeh?'

'No! It's nothing to do with that. It's to do with what was – on it.'

Vinnie turns to face Joey and frowns.

'Go on!' He throws the pencil onto the table and sits into his chair.

'I mean, it wasn't what was on the laptop itself. There was nothing on that. It was what was on one of the USB sticks that was kinda hidden in the bag.'

'Hidden?'

'Yeah, like in a tiny pocket in the side.'

'And?'

'It … it had an awful lot of stuff on it.'

Vinnie stares at him, waiting for him to continue, but Joey feels his throat go dry.

'Will you land the fuckin' plane, Joey!'

Joey lets out a sigh of resignation.

'It was full of photos – of Quinlan and other criminal types. I don't know who any of them are, but you might know. I mean, you might have seen some of them some time in the past.' Joey pauses and feels his face redden. When will this shit with his face stop happening? 'A lot of the stuff on it looks dodgy, and there's figures as well and names and addresses.'

'What do you mean – dodgy?'

Joey nearly smiles, because in Vinnie's world dodgy isn't that bad a word.

'Dodgy – like Quinlan with young girls. Or maybe young boys … I dunno. And drugs. And lots of cash and probably the names of clients or whatever. I don't know. I hardly looked at it, because I was afraid to.'

'And you brought it out with you, to show me – this USB stick thing?'

'No.'

'So where is it?'

'I gave it to this cop.'

'You handed it over to a *cop*? What cop? What the fuck, Joey?'

Joey can't remember if he's already told Vinnie about the cop. He doesn't think he has, but suddenly he's not sure.

'He was a cop that called to see me and Jackie. He said he wanted to bring Quinlan down and maybe you could help because you might have information on him that they could use.'

'And you're only telling me all this now?'

'That's because I wanted to handle it myself, Vinnie. I didn't want to involve you in anything in case you got pulled into shitty stuff and especially after what happened before with … you know … what happened with yer man.'

Vinnie rubs his forehead with all his fingers, and Joey knows he's not happy. Then his hands are down and he's staring at Joey and Joey looks away and rubs at one of his eyes. Vinnie sighs loudly, like maybe he thinks the news isn't really that bad.

'So! You gave this cop all the information they thought I had – that I didn't know I had – and they'll use it now to take down Quinlan. And that's it. All sorted!'

Joey releases a long, loud sigh of his own.

'It's not sorted. I thought it was, but it's not. It's fucked up. The whole thing has got totally – completely – fucked up.'

Vinnie lets out a groan. 'Will you just tell me the rest of it and let me decide whether it's fucked up or not.'

'The cop fucked it up!'

'How?'

'He's crooked or bent or whatever.'

'How do you know he's crooked?'

'Because he's in a lot of the photos himself, the ones on the USB stick. He's up to his eyeballs in shit with Quinlan. He's taking all sorts of drugs and money, and he's with young girls and it's so ... just fucked up.'

Vinnie's fingers are back on his forehead. He gets up and goes to stand by the window that looks down on the workshop. Then he turns to Joey and there's a look in his eyes that says how disappointed he is once more with Joey's decision-making.

'Let me get this straight. You gave all this valuable information that can be used against Quinlan ... to ... a crooked cop, who's up to his eyeballs in all the dodgy stuff Quinlan's involved in?'

'I did it for you, Vinnie. Once I saw what was on the computer stick, I knew what was going on. The cop was worried because he thought you must have found the photos and the figures, and that was why you'd come back. But I knew you hadn't found them, because if you had, you'd never have given me the laptop in the first place. So, I gave him the laptop, pretending I knew nothing, and like you knew nothing either.'

'I'm getting a headache listening to you, Joey.'

'I'm trying to tell you what happened, Vinnie. I'm trying to tell you why I gave him the laptop as well as the USB stick.'

'You gave away the laptop as well?'

'I had to, Vinnie – even though it was just the computer bag he was mad keen on. Like, I could hardly just give him that or he'd have smelled a rat. And Sharon's laptop really was stolen on her, so I wasn't lying about that. Actually, she got it back. But that's a different story, and I was only lying about some of it – well, *not* lying. But the main thing I was doing was keeping you out of it, so everything could get sorted.'

'Tell me you made a few copies of all this stuff.'

'No!' Joey lies, and when he looks towards Vinnie, he sees a small shake of the head, like Vinnie's thinking – same Joey as before, the stupid Joey high on pills and drink who wanted to call an ambulance instead of making a run for it.

'I did it to protect you, Vinnie. I just wanted Quinlan to realise you weren't a threat to any of them. Then they'd leave you alone and you'd be able to come out from hiding. That's what you said you wanted to happen. That's what Ma and Jackie want. And it's what Isabel wants too, more than anything else.'

'What's this cop's name?'

'Doyle. Aidan Doyle. You know the guy?'

'Maybe,' Vinnie says and frowns like he's trying to picture him. 'Could be the guy that everyone thought was from Revenue. Snazzy dresser, in about the place talking to Quinlan in his office like he was checking Quinlan's books.'

'That has to be him, Vinnie! And him and Quinlan were putting me under pressure to tell them where you're living. I thought if I gave them the USB with the photos it'd be all sorted … but … but it's not.'

'So you're saying there's more?'

'Yeah!' Joey answers, feeling suddenly breathless. He knows Vinnie is going to be angry with him and it's not fair. 'I don't know what to do any more,' he says and he can feel his voice going strange on him and he knows there's tears behind both lids just wanting to crash down onto his cheeks.

'What the fuck did you do, Joey?'

'It wasn't me that did it.'

'Will you just tell me what you've done.'

'Weso!'

'What about Weso?'

'He made a copy of everything and sent some of them to Quinlan, threatening to blackmail him – and the cop.'

Vinnie laughs loud like it's a piece of crazy news he's hearing. He comes back towards the table and sits into his chair.

'Weso! Fucking hell! I didn't think he had the balls to go and do something like that.'

He swivels his chair around like he's looking for something and Joey knows it's his smokes. But they're not there, and then it's like he forgets what he's searching for, as he leans an elbow on his calculations and makes another loud laugh that becomes a cough and he splutters like he's going to bring up crap from his chest.

'Weso!'

'But Quinlan doesn't know it's Weso who's sent the photos.'

Vinnie turns his chair to face Joey and his eyes narrow.

'Who does he think sent them?'

'You!'

'Me?'

'Yeah, he thinks you sent them, Vinnie. Weso put the initial 'V' on a letter demanding a hundred grand. I'm thinking he's hoping to be the go-between, and then he'll just fuck off with the money. Or maybe he's concocted some other plan for how he'll end up with the money. Maybe he's going to tell you about it and want to split it with you?'

Vinnie gets to his feet.

'The little bollix!' Vinnie says. 'A hundred grand! The little bollix,' he says again, and goes back over to the window.

Joey can see his head bent and the fingers of one hand covering his eyes like maybe he's taking a break from having to think about how stupid Joey is. Or maybe he's deciding what he's going to do with Weso when he finds him. What's Sharon going to say and how's she going to feel if anything happens to her brother? Even though the sap has brought it on himself.

'What are you going to do, Vinnie?'

He doesn't answer. Now he's rubbing the side of a finger across his mouth like he's deciding on something. He turns and his face has hardened, and Joey feels like he's back on that road in the new estate where they tried to rob the catalytic converter.

'How did Weso get hold of all the info?'

Joey wasn't expecting the question, so he doesn't know what to say. He doesn't want to have to tell the true story because he knows Vinnie isn't really interested.

'No, don't bother telling me, because this is the type of shit that happens with you, Joey.'

'What do you want me to do?' Joey asks. There has to be something he can do to make it up to Vinnie.

'I don't want you to do anything. Do you hear me? You go home and stay out of this mess and I'll sort it out myself. And whatever you do, don't call a fucking ambulance.'

Joey moves towards the door because he doesn't want to show his eyes tearing up.

'You hear me? You do nothing! I'll find this fool Weso and sort it out myself. OK?' Joey has paused and doesn't turn around. 'OK, Joey?' Vinnie says and his voice is softer now. Almost gentle.

Joey nods and then he's gone from the room.

30

Joey does exactly what Vinnie has told him. He's going to work as many hours as they'll give him in the café. Let Vinnie and Weso sort it out themselves because anytime he tries to help he just makes things worse for everyone. He just wants to spend as much time as he can in Tina's café now, and not think.

They don't offer much for breakfast – just coffee and croissants and other pastries. Then it's more solid stuff for lunch like pizza and panini yokes, toasted sandwiches and focaccia. The focaccia is light and airy and moist with olive oil and there's black olives in some of them and amazing little thumbprints that Matteo makes in each one like he's an artist marking his work.

The place is mad busy in the morning and at lunch, but things calm shortly after two, and then it's afternoon coffee and cakes and then the school kids come in, and Tina gives out about them because they take up seats and order sweet fuck-all except for drinking chocolate, or one ice cream with three or four spoons.

When he goes home in the evening he sits talking to Jackie for a while but tries to zone out when the conversation becomes about Vinnie. She's on about his visit to the choir. Poor Vinnie is obviously very lonely. He's missing his family. She's wondering if he'll come back a second time – and what might she say to him? Maybe Joey could go with her and maybe he could sit where Vinnie sat and wait there in case he turns up. And he could talk to Vinnie and tell him that it's OK for him to come back, that whatever happened in the past can be put behind him. And she says it's OK for him to be upset the way he was when he heard the story.

He wants to scream at her to get her to stop talking about Vinnie. What's wrong with her that all she can talk about is Vinnie? Is there still something going on between herself and him that his ma should hear about?

All he can do is tell her he's not feeling well, he has a bug and just needs time on his own. Then he hears her on the phone in her own bedroom and he knows she's talking to his ma and it's all about Vinnie once more.

That's why it feels so comforting to have his hands in a big sink of warm water, scrubbing pots until they shine.

And the next day he's there is even better because Tina has no lectures and has decided to teach him stuff. She shows him how to make an Americano and it's straightforward enough for him to master. But when she moves to showing him how to make a cappuccino, he hangs back from the machine like it might do him harm the way it spits out steam. She can't believe how little confidence he has. Tina is patient with him, though. He likes that about her.

'If you can learn how to make proper coffee and especially decent cappuccinos, you'll never be short of work. Especially if you're good at it and confident – confident, Joey. Do you hear me?'

He fills the jug halfway with milk so that it reaches the 'v' of the jug spout. Then she tells him he has to stretch the milk and he laughs at that and wants to know how you stretch milk. Is it similar to how his ma stretches money? She submerges the metal nozzle just below the surface of the milk and gives it a five-second blast of steam to create air bubbles. He watches closely and he feels her side touch his own and the smell of the coffee mixes with the smell of the shampoo she uses like it's apples or some sort of fruit and it's difficult to concentrate and he wants her to step back so he can, but he doesn't want that to happen either, so he says nothing. She dips the nozzle another half a centimetre, so it creates a little whirlpool motion, and she lets it spin until the milk heats up. Then she takes the milk away from the steam and wipes the nozzle lovingly with a small blue cloth to remove any drips. He leans his side against her and she bumps him away and tells him to concentrate. He has a joke about getting steamed up but doesn't know how to make it the way it will sound funny, so he stays silent.

He watches her now as she knocks the jug gently off the worktop and then swirls it before she pours it into the coffee. She says it's to remove any big bubbles and it also helps to keep the foam and milk together. He loves the sound of her voice and her quiet concentration, as she gently holds a white cup in one hand, just out from her chin, and slowly pours the milk, then stops, then pours, then stops once more, and finishes it all with a milky coffee-brown drawing of a beautiful heart shape on top. She turns to him then and offers it to him.

He takes a cautious taste out of it and smiles at her. Then he gulps it.

'For God's sake, Joey! You have to sip it!' she says like he's a hopeless case.

He puts two fingers in the cup to drag out the brown foam at the bottom because it's what he likes best and can't bear to see it wasted. She groans and shakes her head.

That's when his phone rings and he surrenders the empty cup and moves towards the front of the café to take the call. It's Sharon's name on the screen. He turns back towards the coffee machine, and Tina is there watching him like maybe she knows who's calling and she's waiting now to see how he deals with it.

'Joey! Have you seen my brother?'

'No. Why?'

'My ma rang me to say he called to the house last night looking for his passport. She wasn't even sure he had a passport but he had. What's going on, Joey?'

'I don't know, Sharon. I don't have anything to do with him since he took up with Quinlan.'

'Is he in trouble, Joey?'

'Maybe he just wants a holiday away.'

'He doesn't do holidays.'

'I don't know what's going on. But he's old enough to take care of himself.'

'No, he's not. He was never able. And Ma is worried now because she didn't like the shifty way he was acting, like he wouldn't tell her anything.'

'Come on, Sharon, he never told any of yous anything. And yous were better off not knowing.'

Luca comes out from the kitchen with a pot in his hand and he points to the contents and loudly gives out about something that sounds like it's been burned, like it's Tina's fault. And Tina is taking none of it from him and gives as good as she's getting. Then Matteo is behind Luca and he's now waving his arms about and letting him know that he wants him back in the kitchen.

'Are you still there, Joey?'

'Yeah, I'm here.'

'Where exactly are you? Like, what's going on? And you never put in a word with Hazel like you said you would. Cos when I go round to talk to her about working some hours, she tells me you've gone to work in some café. Like, what café? Where is it?'

Joey takes a breath but he doesn't get a chance to answer.

'Oh my God! You're in Tina's. I knew it. I just knew it.'

And then she cuts the call and he's left there, looking at his phone, and then at Tina, who just shakes her head at him and retreats into the kitchen.

His phone rings almost immediately and he hopes it will be Sharon giving him a chance to explain. But it's not Sharon's name on the screen. It's Jackie's.

'Have you seen the news?'

'What news?'

'The shooting!'

'What shooting?'

'There was a shooting. A man's body was found in the sand dunes out at Dollymount Strand. He was shot in the head.'

'But why are you calling me, Jackie? People get shot all the time.'

'Could it be Vinnie?'

Joey didn't think so. He thinks instead of Weso lying cold in some sandy hollow.

'Don't be stupid, Jackie. Why would it be Vinnie?'

'I just have a feeling. I don't know why, but I just have a feeling that something bad is going to happen – if it hasn't happened already. I have it since that cop guy came here, and I felt it worse after that little pup came into the off-licence and broke that wine bottle on the floor. I'm afraid it's Vinnie, Joey.'

Now Joey is afraid. She's put the thought in his head and now it's Vinnie's body that he imagines lying there in the wet sand.

'I'm on my way home,' Joey says, and he leaves the café without a word to anyone, though he knows it'll only be Tina who'll wonder why he left without saying goodbye.

31

He's afraid of the news that might be awaiting him so gets off at the Green and walks down Grafton Street, keeping an eye all the way for any sign of the scooter heads. But when he gets to O'Connell Bridge, he sees two of them in their hoodies and black runners and tracksuit bottoms, like they're twins. They're not interested in him. They're giving grief to a homeless man who's sitting on the footpath, his back against the bridge wall.

One of them has put his scooter leaning against the parapet while he bends down and pokes at the old guy, like he's curious to see what he has hidden in his collection of jackets. Joey can see it's a small terrier too frightened to bark. Joey also sees the boy has two of his fingers strapped together.

He pulls his own hoodie up around his head and runs towards the two lads and grabs the abandoned scooter and raises it above his head like he's weight-lifting.

'Hey! Put that down.'

The lad is standing now, glaring at Joey and forgetting all about the dog. The other lad does nothing except snigger like he's finding it hilarious.

'Yeah, I will,' Joey says, and he flings it over the side of the bridge and into the water, where he can hear it splash.

The lads dart to the wall and Joey also goes to look. He smiles when he sees the scooter dip and drown. Then the lads are glaring at him, but Joey isn't afraid of them.

'Come on!' he screams at them. 'Come on!' And he makes his hands into fists and lunges at the nearest lad, who backs away, scared. And the lad who still has his scooter turns and scoots away across the road, laughing as he goes.

'You bastard!' the abandoned lad shouts, not at Joey, but at his pal, and then he's away across the road after him like he wants to do him harm.

Joey watches to make sure they're gone and then hears what sounds like applause. It is applause and it's coming from a pair of auld ones who have been passing and witnessed the whole thing.

'Little gurriers!' one of the women says and Joey nods in agreement, then nods down at the old man who gives him a grateful thumbs-up.

Then Joey is away, feeling much better with himself and ready for whatever news Jackie has heard in the meantime.

When he gets to Jackie's place there's a black BMW outside her door that he doesn't recognise. He peers in through the side window and sees a metal music stand lying on the back seat. Martin must have bought a new car.

Jackie runs to him and hugs him close.

'What's wrong? Is it Vinnie that was shot?' he asks as soon as she's pulled away from him.

'It's that cop that was here,' Jackie says.

'The cop?'

'Yer man – Doyle. That's who they're saying it is, and they wouldn't be releasing his name if they weren't sure.'

Joey doesn't know what to say or do. He stares blankly at Jackie and then at Martin.

'What's going on, Joey?'

Joey can't seem to find his voice. The crooked cop has been shot. Did Vinnie do it? Joey gave him the cop's name. He shouldn't have done that. But why would Vinnie kill him? Vinnie doesn't kill people. It has to be Quinlan. Quinlan's done it, because it's bad enough having one guy out there with the goods on him without having to worry about a second. So Quinlan has probably got the USB with all the photos, got it off the cop's body. But he must think he still has Vinnie to deal with – though really it's Weso. Is the killing of the cop a message for Vinnie? Or is it a message for Joey because of where the body was found? What the fuck!

'What's going on, Joey?' It's Martin who's asking the question now.

Joey glances at him. Why has she involved this guy in their family shit?

'I don't know what's going on,' Joey says.

'But what has it to do with Vinnie?' Jackie asks.

'I don't know. It could have something – but I don't know.'

'This Doyle man said your stepfather has something belonging to this guy Quinlan,' Martin says, like he's part of the family.

'What did you tell him all that for?' Joey says to Jackie, feeling his blood rise again.

'I have to tell someone and I don't want to be talking to your ma or she'll only be worrying about you – and Vinnie.'

'For fucksake, Jackie, the less anyone knows about everything the safer everyone will be.'

'What do you mean?' Martin asks.

'What do I mean?' Joey's not sure exactly what he means but he knows things will move faster now. 'Look! I don't know exactly what's going on. But I think Vinnie might get pulled into it, even though it's got nothing to do with him.'

'Then you need to go to the guards about it, Joey,' Jackie says. We should have gone there ages ago.'

'We did go there,' Joey says. 'Or they came here. But that cop that got shot was bent. So how am I going to go to the station now and say what I know? How do I know Quinlan hasn't got at other cops in there?'

'But he said he was trying to take Quinlan down,' Jackie says. 'He can't be bent.'

'You can't believe everything everyone tells you, Jackie. He was bent, and Quinlan's probably killed him because he knew too much.'

'Are you safe?' Martin asks. And then he looks with concern at Jackie. 'Is Jackie? And is this anything to do with that little gurrier who tried to intimidate her in my shop?'

'Tried? He *did* intimidate me,' Jackie says.

'We should go straight to the Garda station,' Martin says.

Joey gives Jackie a stare. The way her eyes are darting in her head is telling him she's thinking seriously about it.

'Jackie, you can't go to the guards now. You tell them anything about that cop calling in here and they'll have me and you in there for questioning. And what if Quinlan hears about that? You know how they treat rats. And then the cops will go looking for Vinnie and they'll pull him in. Then they'll start thinking maybe it's Vinnie who's killed the cop. And with his record he's not going to stand a chance.'

'His stepfather has a record?' Martin says suddenly to Jackie. 'You never told me that.'

'Oh, for God's sake. It's all small potatoes!' Jackie says.

'What kind of record?' Martin is putting the question to Joey.

Jackie gets up and moves to get her wine glass where she left it over near the window.

'It's none of your business, Martin. It's not my stepda you're trying to shag.'

'Joey!' Jackie barks at him from over by the window.

Martin turns and stares at her accusingly. 'Jesus, what kind of family am I getting involved with?'

Joey comes to stand in front of the couch and he's in between the pair of them.

'There's no need to be going all drama queen, Martin. You met Vinnie already. Didn't you even invite him to join your choir?'

Martin gasps. 'That man was ... was Vinnie? That man in my church! You said he was just a friend.'

'Yeah! So what?' Jackie says. You told him you needed more male voices. And since when did it become your church, Martin?'

Martin opens his mouth to speak but no words come.

'I think you should go, Martin,' Jackie says, and she turns her back to him and takes a sip of wine from her glass.

Joey eyes Martin all the way as he heads for the door.

'I thought it was going to be Vinnie! I was sure it was Vinnie,' Joey says and now he can't stop the build-up of tears that seem to be flooding his eyes. He puts the backs of his fingers up against them but he knows it's a pointless gesture.

Jackie places her wine glass on the coffee table and then comes to him and puts her arms around him and pulls him closer than she's ever held him before. He's not sure if this is what he wants, or needs, but he lets his head fall against her shoulder as she wraps him in her two arms. He sighs and feels the comfort of her soft fingers on the back of his head and then he closes his eyes and lets the tears flow freely down his face.

32

Joey watches the door as a group of people make their way out of Father Frank's Parish Centre. There's six of them and they're all wrapped up in hooded coats and jackets because there's a biting cold wind now coming in from the sea. They divide up into two groups and get into two cars and he turns his back and bends away from them as they pass behind him and exit. He waits until both cars have disappeared from sight before he makes his way up to the priest's door.

There's a bell, which he rings. Then he steps back. The door is opened by Father Frank and he has a scarf in his hand.

'Oh!' is all he says when he sees Joey standing there. 'I thought it was – well, one of the ladies who forgot her scarf.'

He stands there with the door held in one hand. A phone goes off from somewhere inside.

'I need to get that,' the priest says and he turns and leaves Joey.

Joey stands there and hears the voice but can't make out any of the conversation. Then the priest appears with the phone to his ear and he motions to Joey to come in and he points him towards a door to the side. Then he heads off once more to continue his call.

The room Joey enters is quite bare. There's new carpet on the floor, a plain greyish blue. There's a coffee table in the middle of the room with seven chairs round it. There's a teapot on the table with a knitted Jesus tea-cosy on it. There are seven used mugs and a plate with plain biscuits and small Kit Kats on it. He glances at the walls. There's very little there except for some boring family photos.

The only other item of interest in the room is a table in one corner that's covered with books. When he goes to have a look, he sees one of the books has Father Frank's face on the cover like he wrote it. He takes it in his hand like he's weighing it.

'Sorry about that, Joey. I had to take that call. Someone trying to arrange a funeral.' He doesn't ask Joey to sit nor does he take a seat himself. 'Now! What can I do for you?'

Joey puts the book down and lets his eyes roam once more about the room.

'Do you want to sit down?'

Joey glances at the chairs.

'No,' he says. He doesn't need to sit because he won't be staying long.

'Georgina's daughter, Amber, got your letter by the way.'

The letter? Then he remembers and feels his cheeks burn.

'I presume it was from you?'

Joey doesn't answer and he's not sure where to look.

'I'll take that as a "yes", then,' the priest says.

Joey nods.

'Do you need to talk about it?'

The question takes Joey by surprise. He doesn't want to talk about it. It's not the reason he's here.

'Did they show you what I wrote?'

'No, and I didn't ask. It's none of my business.'

'Yeah,' Joey says.

Father Frank sits. Joey is still standing, and everything feels awkward, like it's still his turn to talk.

'So, what can I do for you, Joey?'

Joey sighs like he's not sure about what he needs to do.

'Is this where you have your meetings?'

'Yes. You just missed one.'

Joey takes two brown envelopes out of his pocket. One of them is small and flat; the other is large and fat. He hands both to the priest. Father Frank stares at the envelopes but doesn't take either.

'The big one has money in it,' Joey says.

'Money?'

'Money I saved.'

'Money you saved. And now you want to give it away.'

'Yeah.'

'Why?'

'Because of how I got it.'

It's also because he knows it's what Sharon would have wanted him to do.

'From ...'

'Yeah!' Joey doesn't need to let him finish the sentence. 'There's one thousand four hundred and sixty euro in there.'

Father Frank stares at the envelope.

'And what am I to do with it?'

'Maybe give it to ... Georgina ... for her daughter. Or you could give it to whoever you think needs it. I don't want it anyway.'

Joey places the big envelope on the table. Father Frank stares at it like he's unsure what to do next. Then his phone rings in his pocket and he pulls it clear and looks at the screen.

'I have to take this, Joey,' he says and leaves the room.

Joey places the smaller envelope beside the large one. The small one has 'Detective Brady' written in block letters on the front of it and it has nothing inside but a USB stick. He lied to Vinnie about that, said he hadn't copied what was on the USB that was in the computer bag, but he couldn't tell him the truth or Vinnie would have made him hand it over. Then Joey quietly leaves the room and the priest's house with the door ajar behind him.

It's well dark now and the street lights aren't great in this part of town. The shops are shuttered and there's an air of gloom about the deserted streets. The wind that's followed him in from the coast seems to have turned colder.

He goes to open the gate, then notices the van just up from where he's standing and the back door is open ready to load ... something. Then he sees the three hoodies – they're bigger lads than the usual but they're wearing balaclavas and he knows they're coming for him. He's been expecting it, and part of him is wondering why it's taken so long. He puts his hands up as they approach to show he's willing to go wherever they want to take him. The first lad grabs him by the collar of his jacket and he doesn't see the Taser, just feels the sudden shock that shoots through every bone and nerve in his body. He tries to fall, but is held up. He's wearing his hoodie. This is what happens when he's back to wearing hoodies.

33

There's a desk in front of Joey and a man in a Garda cap stands behind it. He must be in a Garda station, he thinks. The man takes off the cap and smiles, showing off two rows of white teeth. It's Quinlan. Is he a cop too?

'Joey,' he cries out like he and Joey are best buds who haven't seen one another in years. 'Sit down! Sit down!'

Joey feels a chair pushed against the back of his legs and he has no option but to sit. 'And ta very much for the spondulicks. That was very nice of you, Joey. And the holiday snaps. Very much appreciated. But that's not what people are watching these days, Joey.'

And then Joey notices that Quinlan has a priest's collar on him and he realises it's not Quinlan any more. It's Father Frank.

He stands out of the way and it's like Joey is back in that church and he's sitting where Vinnie must have sat and he's staring up towards the altar where Martin has gathered a choir together. They're all there. Ma is there.

And Jackie. Isabel is crying her eyes out and Georgina and her daughter look like they have no more tears left to cry. They're all gazing into a laptop screen and Joey thinks they're looking at all the photos that are to be seen on the USB. But then they turn their eyes towards where he's sitting and he has to gasp for breath.

It's not the USB pics they've been watching. It's the CCTV footage of him, Vinnie and Weso. They won't stop staring with those eyes boring into him and he feels his cheeks ablaze like he's a candle being lit. He must escape! He has to escape – must get away from all those accusing eyes that are making his face burn. But he can't escape. Something is stopping him. He's a candle that's melting and the wax is sticking him like glue to where he's standing. Sitting. He tries to move his legs, but they won't budge. He attempts to lift his arms but they won't obey.

He opens his eyes and is now wide awake.

He sees Ginsey McGinn sitting in a wooden armchair like the one he's sitting in himself. Ginsey's head has dropped down onto his chest like he has dozed off. His long black fringe is hanging down so he can't see his face. It's greasy, but Ginsey's hair is never any other way. Joey thinks about getting up and away, except he can't budge. He sees why. His wrists have been tethered to the armrests with black plastic ties. He leans his head to the side and can see they have done the same to his ankles. He twists his shoulders and pushes both knees against the side of the chair and he can hear it creak in protest. He's all tied up like an oven-ready chicken.

The room he's in is like some sort of narrow bar with dirty wooden floorboards the size of planks. It feels like an old basement dive that's no longer in business. He's reminded of the bar he and Stephen were sculling pints in that night, except this bar is L-shaped and goes two-thirds of the length of the room. He's at the top of the L. There's a carpeted stairway with wooden bannisters across from the other end of the bar and it seems like it's the only way in or out of the place. The side of the room across from the bar is lined with four mahogany tables with more of the wooden armchairs pressed in against them. It's like a saloon in a cowboy film.

The bar counter is covered with a selection of empty beer bottles and dirty ashtrays and a sprinkling of empty crisp bags, as if the bar had to close before any cleaning up could be done. On the stretch of bar nearest him lies a Dublin GAA scarf and woolly hat. Behind the bar he can see that two of the mirrors have been cracked and the spirit bottles on the shelves in front of them look like they're in need of dusting. Down the other end he can hear voices. He leans his head to the side and can see three of Quinlan's hoods sitting on bar stools and eating takeaway McDonald's off a pool table. There are white panels of wood that could be pieces of bedside lockers resting on the pool table like it's an IKEA jigsaw. They're not paying any attention to his end of the bar so he looks away from them and takes stock of his own situation.

He shifts in his seat, trying to loosen the ties, but he knows it's hopeless and the creaking he makes just causes him pain – and wakens his captor.

Ginsey raises his head and pulls aside the greasy curtains of hair and tucks them in behind his ears. Then he stares at Joey like he's been dreaming too and is now trying to place himself in the real world. He's got a gun nesting on his lap. For fucksake! His hands had been covering it but now they're up rubbing at his eyes. He glances down when he catches Joey staring at it. Ginsey grins, revealing his two crooked front teeth, and lifts the gun up. It's snug in his grip like he's used to holding it.

'My little Glock!' he says and laughs and waves it in the air. Then his laugh turns into a sneer and he points the gun at Joey's groin area.

Joey stares down at his jeans and sees the stain where he's wet himself.

'You're not so fuckin' smart now! Are yeh?' Ginsey takes out his phone and takes a quick snap of his prisoner.

'What the fuck are yeh doing?' The voice is Quinlan's and it comes from somewhere behind Joey, like there's a door back there that Quinlan has come through.

Ginsey quickly stashes the phone in his pocket.

'I said what the fuck are yeh doing, yeh stupid prick? You making a record for the cops so they know you were involved? Why don't you have me in it as well? Yeah?'

'Fuck, I never thought of that, Mr Quinlan.' He retrieves the phone from his pocket and quickly deletes the photo.

'And I thought I told you to call me as soon as he came to.'

Quinlan's voice is closer now and Joey doesn't like the way it sounds. He feels thick fingers take a grip on the back of his neck and then the fingers squeeze into the muscle and bone.

'Didn't think it was necessary to use a Taser, Joey,' he says, as he rests his palm on the top of Joey's head and then combs Joey's fringe out of his eyes with his fingers. 'They said you were ready to come along without a fight, but I suppose if you give young lads these gadgets, they just have to use them to see if they work properly.'

Quinlan has got rid of his business look. He's wearing blue jeans and a denim shirt open at the neck to reveal his bare chest. He stands staring down at Joey with his thumbs lodged in the big brown belt that he's wearing. It's got a bronze buckle the size of a gate on it. He's wearing a pair of brown slip-on boots with thick leather soles. All that's missing is a gun and holster.

'You going line dancing, Mr Quinlan?' Joey says.

The comment doesn't seem to bother Quinlan, but Ginsey's amused.

'What the fuck you smiling at?' Quinlan barks at Ginsey's head, pulling one of his hands clear of his belt and balling it into a fist.

'Since when did you start giving crazies like Ginsey here the use of a gun? Joey says. 'You trying to get someone killed?'

Ginsey jumps to his feet with the gun in hand as if he'd like nothing better now than to pistol-whip Joey into shutting up. Joey can't help but smile at the reaction, though he knows it's not the wisest move he can make.

'Will you sit down, Ginsey,' says Quinlan. 'You're all over the fuckin' shop.'

Ginsey sits with a puss on him. He glares at Joey, like this is being added to the list of things Joey has done to piss him off.

The lads with the McDonald's come up the bar to have a gander at what's going on, but Quinlan barks at them and sends them scurrying back to their food and the puzzle he's set them, fixing those lockers.

'So! I presume we're waiting for Vinnie to arrive?' Joey says like it's an announcement.

'You fuckin' betcha,' Ginsey says and points the gun at his own head.

'Yeah, that's the idea, Ginsey. You go and shoot yourself before Vinnie gets here and rips the head off yeh,' says Joey.

Ginsey is ready to point the gun in a new direction, but one look from Quinlan makes him hesitate.

'Will you put that gun down, you stupid dickhead. Can't you see he's just trying to rile you?'

'Well, he's fuckin' succeeding, and if he says anything else to me, he's going to get the taste of this barrel in his mouth.'

'For fucksake, Ginsey,' says Quinlan. Don't make my job here more difficult than it is. Keep all your pent-up hate for Vinnie. Remember what the fucker did to you.'

Joey can see from the glazed look in Ginsey's eyes he's still quite high on some sort of gear or maybe he's coming down from it. Joey knows that look only too well.

'I know what's going on here,' Joey says. 'You want Ginsey –'

But he doesn't get a chance to finish the sentence because Quinlan slaps him hard across the face. Joey gets such a shock he feels the tears gather in the corner of his eyes. He lowers his head and grunts a pathetic protest as he struggles in a hopeless attempt to get out of the chair.

'Vinnie won't come,' he shouts in anger down to the wooden floorboards. 'He won't because we're not family no more.'

He feels Quinlan's hand grab him by his hair and his head is forced upwards.

'For your sake he'd better,' Quinlan says and pushes Joey's head away from him and then he walks off down the length of the bar like he's remembered something more important than hurting Joey.

'What the fuck. Will ye get back and fix those fucking lockers?' he barks at the three lads.

'We're just finishing our food, Mr Quinlan.'

'Yous are like children with yer slurping. I can't bear that sound. And for fucksake, start eating decent food for a change.'

He doesn't wait for their answer but moves closer to them, as if to check on what progress they've made in whatever task he's given them. Joey glances now at Ginsey and sees him take a tab of something from his pocket and put it in his mouth. Then he dips to the side and takes up a bottle of water and gulps it down, then crushes the plastic and flings it behind him.

'I never asked Vinnie to hurt you, Ginsey. I didn't. I wouldn't have done that, even though I was out of my head half the time.'

'Yeah, sure!'

'And that day out near the Luas stop – that *was* Vinnie. But I got him to leave you alone. Remember how scared you were?'

'I wasn't scared, so shut the fuck up,' Ginsey says, trying to keep his voice low.

'I'm just saying, Ginsey. I know what it's like – you know, to be scared.' Joey nods towards his own wet crotch. 'I'm sorry, Ginsey. For what it's worth. I'm sorry.'

'Yeah, sure!' Ginsey says, keeping an eye on what's going on down the other end of the bar like he's been left out of something important.

'Am I just the bait, then?' Joey says.

Ginsey grins. 'Yeah. You're one big maggot.'

'What's he going to do with me, Ginsey? Because I'm going to witness whatever Quinlan has planned for Vinnie. And what about you, Ginsey? I know where this is all heading and why he's got you here.'

Quinlan is striding back towards them so Ginsey goes quiet.

'Fuckin' amateurs.'

'You've got all this wrong, Mr Quinlan,' Joey says.

Quinlan eyes him.

'You've got it all wrong. Like … this has nothing to do with Vinnie at all. I don't know where you got that idea from. I know you heard he was coming back to Dublin, but he was never coming back to cause trouble. He just came back to try and mend things with his family. Like, I don't know why you think he's out to get you.'

Quinlan pulls out one of the saloon chairs from the nearest table and pushes it towards Joey; then he sits into it.

'You know ... I liked Vinnie,' Quinlan says now. 'I really liked him. Me and him got on. But I never really trusted him. There was always that look in his eye that said he wanted what I had and he wouldn't mind taking it off me instead of grafting for it.'

'He is grafting for it,' Joey says. 'He is. And it isn't him that's blackmailing you because I'd know. He's never even seen what was on –'

Joey stops talking. Quinlan is staring at him.

'What was on...? Go on!'

'What was on that USB stick. He never saw any of the photos. I saw them. I was the one who saw them, but I pretended to your crooked cop that I hadn't, because I knew he was the one who was freaking out, and he was the one who was making you freak out also. But it's not Vinnie that's blackmailing you. It's not.'

Ginsey sniggers and turns to the side and spits like there's a bad taste in his mouth.

'Will you stop that fuckin' disgusting habit,' Quinlan snaps at him.

'What? Like this place is a five star.'

'Just fuckin' stop it or you'll be spitting out teeth – what's left of them.'

Ginsey lowers his eyes and wipes his mouth with the back of one hand.

'It's not Vinnie!' Joey says again.

'Sure! I've heard that story already and nearly believed it. But then some of those photos arrive. And who else could they be from but Vinnie?'

'I'm telling you! Someone else is behind it. Maybe it was Doyle who made copies and gave them to one of his crooked pals.'

'We'll find out soon enough when Vinnie gets here.'

'What are you going to do? Kill him? And then what? What about me? You kill Vinnie, I'll know you've done it.'

'You won't talk, Joey. And you know how I know that? You won't say a word because you know how these things work. You'll keep your mouth shut because you've got a mother you need to protect. And a sister. And you've a girl you're keen on. I'm not talking about Sharon, but that young one from that little Italian place. And you've an aunt you quite like too. I quite like her myself to tell you the truth. Will I keep going on?'

Joey is too stunned to talk. He can only sigh. He lets his head fall onto his chest.

A door opens at the top of the stairs and they all turn to look and see another of Quinlan's boys come running down the steps. His hoodie is down so they can all see the sunken eyes and the pale spotty face that's full of panic. But it's not a boy. It's a girl. Her hair is short. He can see that now and the hooped ear-ring in one of her ears. She glances down towards the lads at the end of the room like whatever she's going to announce is going to upset them also.

Joey thinks it's about Vinnie. Vinnie has arrived and he's lurking upstairs somewhere. He tries to free his hands but it's another hopeless effort.

'What's going on, Joy?' Quinlan shouts towards the girl.

'It's not my fault, Mr Quinlan. It's not.'

'Just tell me what the fuck is going on,' Quinlan says, moving towards the girl who has decided to stay on the bottom step like it's for her safety or maybe she's not allowed down here.

'Your safe in the office is wide open and the money I counted yesterday is gone. And your car's gone too.'

Quinlan stops in his tracks. Joey sees his body tense and his two hands up either side of his head like he's afraid it's going to explode.

'What do you mean – gone?'

'The money in the safe. It's gone. The safe door is wide open and your car is gone from outside. Weso's after driving off in it.'

Quinlan lets out an animal roar, then runs for the stairs and Joy dodges out of his way before he can knock her aside. He thumps up the steps and moves a lot faster than Joey would have thought he could move. The three lads at the end of the room stop what they've been doing and they stand and their eyes are on the stairs waiting for the return of their boss. Joy stays where she is, blinking, like this is the first time she's been down here. She goes to put a foot on the bottom step like she's thinking she should go back up and explain, but she doesn't get a chance because now they can see Quinlan's leather-soled boots coming back down the steps and they can hear him swear like every step is a fresh curse and they're all aimed at Weso.

'Should I call the guards?' Joy asks, and she's staring at the three lads like they might know the answer – and then at Quinlan.

Ginsey lets out a shriek of laughter. Joey stares at him, glares at him like what the fuck is he trying to do. Is he trying to get himself killed? But Ginsey is doubling over with the fun he sees in all this.

He points at the girl.

'Yeah, Joy, call the cops.' He bends over once more like he's got stomach cramps but the three lads show blank faces like they can read the situation a bit better than Ginsey. But Quinlan is not paying them any attention because he's coming towards Ginsey now and his eyes are on fire with hate.

'What the fuck!' he roars, and Ginsey stops suddenly and straightens himself to wipe tears away from his eyes.

Quinlan's right in front of him, his eyes still ablaze. 'I told you to keep an eye on Weso. He was your responsibility, you little piece of shit.'

'You shouldn't talk to me like that, Mr Quinlan. You really shouldn't,' he says, and he has the gun now in his hand and he's pointing it at Quinlan's stomach.

'I'll talk to you any way I like, you little rat-faced pimple.'

Ginsey's face contorts with a mixture of anger and hurt.

'It's your own fault, you stupid fuck!' Ginsey shouts. 'I told you Weso would screw you over but you wouldn't listen. You won't listen to anyone, cos you're just a big baldy piece of shit.'

Quinlan moves in closer with his thick fist raised like a hammer.

'You give me that gun or I'll make you eat it,' Quinlan snarls and makes a grab for it.

The shot when it comes takes everyone by surprise – especially Quinlan. He lets his hands fall away to his sides and he looks at the puncture in his belly. He stares at it in shock.

Ginsey stares at it also, from where he's sitting, looking dazed, in his chair.

Joey stares at it and then sees the blood ooze to stain the denim. There is a weird kind of silence now, like time has become frozen or a picture has been paused. Quinlan's hands both go to the stain and his two thumbs and fingers circle it like he might be able to contain it in the heart shape he makes. But he needs to stay standing for that to work and he's suddenly not able. He staggers backwards against the counter, his elbows behind him on the bar, standing there like he's shooting the breeze. Then his feet give way and his back slips down along the bar rail and he crumples and folds up in a heap at the base of the bar.

Joey stares at him and knows he's dead.

He hears movement, and when he looks towards the stairs he can see Joy disappearing out the top of it, and the three lads have their hoodies up to cover their faces, and they stare at the dead body on the wooden floor and then at Ginsey and at the gun, and all three make the same decision at the same time – and they're gone racing up the stairs and out of sight.

Ginsey stands now and stares at the gun in his hand.

'I told you!' he calls out to the lifeless body on the ground. 'I fuckin' told you not to talk to me like that, but you wouldn't listen.'

He turns away from the body and from Joey and rubs at his forehead with one hand and holds the gun down by his side with the other.

'Hey, let me out of here, Ginsey,' Joey cries.

Ginsey turns to look at him like he's puzzled that Joey is still there.

'You heard him! You heard the disrespectful way he spoke to me?'

'Yeah, Ginsey, I did. And the gun went off accidentally.'

Ginsey stares at the gun.

'It didn't!' He laughs down at it and Joey wonders if he's completely losing it now and whatever tab he took has taken him to some crazy place.

'You need to get out of here, Ginsey. You need to get out of here fast. That shot – people will have heard the shot and someone will call the cops.'

Ginsey stares at Joey as if he's trying to establish who exactly Joey is. Then he leans down as though to inspect the lifeless body of Quinlan.

'I shot him? I actually fuckin' shot him?'

'You did, Ginsey.'

'Fucker had it coming!'

'Yeah, Ginsey! He did. He absolutely did. But you need to get away outta here.'

Ginsey turns to examine Joey once more and his glazed eyes move from Joey's face to the black ties that hold his wrists to the arms of the chair.

'You can leave me here, Ginsey! You can! Just go! Just go and I'll say I didn't see anything. Get that football hat on the counter there and push it down over my head and it'll be like how could I have seen anything? I promise you I won't say anything because I owe you one. I owe you for what Vinnie did to you.'

Ginsey eyes the football scarf and hat. He goes to the counter and pokes at the hat with the barrel of the gun. He lifts it off and then takes it in his hands. He laughs at it, then comes towards Joey and pushes it all the way down over his head to just below his nose.

'He had it coming to him, Ginsey,' Joey says into the darkness. 'Now get out of here.'

He hears Ginsey move down the bar. Then there's noise from upstairs like someone is moving about. Joey listens. He can't hear Ginsey and maybe it is Ginsey already up there. But then Joey's heart sinks at the sound of his name being called.

'Joey!' It's Vinnie's voice. 'Joey!' The voice is calling louder and he hears footsteps in front of him and he knows it's Ginsey scurrying back towards where he is sitting. He wants to shout to warn Vinnie but knows he can't do that either. He twists and turns in the chair trying to topple it over but gets a sudden slap across the top of his head.

'Stop moving or it'll be the gun you feel,' Ginsey hisses.

Joey goes still. Then he hears his name being called again.

'Vinnie!' Joey shouts back.

'That's right! You call him down.'

Joey shuts up. He can't believe what he's done. But he knows Vinnie will come down those steps anyway. He can hear Ginsey's panting breath behind him. He feels the cold steel tip of the barrel on his scalp.

'Call him again!' Ginsey hisses, but no way Joey is going to obey. 'Doesn't fuckin' matter – here he comes now.'

'Joey!' Vinnie's voice calls. He's at the top of the stairs. There is silence from above now, like Vinnie is waiting for a response.

'No, Vinnie! No!' Joey shouts and he feels the impact of the butt of the gun against his skull. He wants to put a hand up to the pain but he can't. He can't even think about the pain now because he knows Vinnie is coming further into the room.

'Stay where you are, Vinnie! Please!' Joey cries expecting another blow on the head but none comes.

'What are you going to do with that, Vinnie?' Ginsey snarls. 'You gonna stick me with it, are yeh? You might have scared me twice but you're not going to do it a third time!'

'You little prick. What the fuck are you after doing here?'

'I shot him. But he made me shoot him. And I don't give a fuck that he's dead because he deserved it. What's one more arsehole less in the world.'

'You need to put that gun down, Ginsey. You need to put it down before you do more harm here.'

'Just go, Vinnie,' Joey pleads. 'Please! Just go.'

'Put it down, Ginsey!'

Joey gets a fright because Vinnie's voice is closer now, and over the mad pouding of his own heart, he can hear Ginsey moving out in front of him. He tries to rattle himself loose on the chair but it's useless.

'Just go, Vinnie! Go!' Joey pleads once more, but Vinnie doesn't seem to be heeding him.

'You're gonna have to kill me too then, Ginsey,' Vinnie says. 'Are you able for that, you little prick? I can see your hand shaking.'

'Yeah, it's shaking like a bitch but that won't stop me putting a bullet in his thick skull. And maybe I'll do that before putting one in yours.'

Joey hears Ginsey drag his feet nearer to him, and then he feels the tight hand-hold on his hair and the tug feels like it's going to tear a clump of it from his head.

'No, Vinnie! No! He's not going to do it!' Joey cries out, and the sound he hears now is a shout from Vinnie as he charges towards them.

The sound of the shot this time hurts Joey's right ear – and he struggles furiously with the chair but it won't release him. He stops struggling and his ear is sore and sounds are muffled now as he tries to figure out what's happened. He keeps his head still and waits to hear Vinnie's voice say he has the gun, and he's waiting to hear Ginsey's footsteps on the stairs. He does hear running and it sounds like Ginsey's hurried steps.

'Vinnie?' Joey calls out. 'Vinnie!'

He feels fingers grab hold of the woollen hat and it's dragged clear of his head.

Vinnie! Vinnie has the hat and he's smiling at Joey.

'I didn't have you down as a Dubs fan,' he says. But there's something wrong, something catching his breath like his voice isn't working properly.

'Vinnie!' is all Joey can say.

Vinnie places one hand gently on Joey's cheek. 'I'm sorry! I'm sorry, bud,' he says and his fingers slip, then crawl down Joey's cheek like he's drawing lines on his face, and slowly, so slowly like he's melting, Vinnie collapses and sinks to the floor.

'DA!' Joey screams. 'DA!' He screams it so loud it almost blocks out the sirens sounding from the street above them.

34

Ma is holding onto Jackie, gripping the back of her coat like she's afraid she's going to slip into the open grave. Jackie has her arm around her, squeezing her close. Joey is beside his ma. She hasn't let go of the tight grip she's had on his arm since they arrived at the church.

Joey looks behind him and can see Tina wiping tears away from her eyes. She never met Vinnie, but she will hear enough stories now to make up for that. Luca is with her and he's glad about that. And Sharon is there and Stephen has had to put his arm around her because she started crying into his shoulder. Sharon and Stephen? Who ever would have thought it? Least of all Stephen. Miles and Rodney are standing behind Sharon, and Richie from the shop is next to them blocking out daylight. It'll be a coffin as big as a boat they'll need when he goes.

There's a crowd gathered about them in the grave-yard, most of them are probably rubbernecking because of the story. Martin is there but keeping his distance from Jackie like he's not sure if he's going to be part of this family, or if he wants to be. There's some of the lads from his school that he hardly knows any more. And there's the neighbours and people from the community centre that he knows to see but has never spoken to.

Weso isn't there. Nobody knows where Weso is, and Sharon feels ashamed, so he hasn't asked her anything about him. Quinlan's car – the one Weso took – was found at the airport, and he's probably on some beach or in some bar. And Ginsey McGinn isn't there either because he's in prison, awaiting trial.

The sky is one grey cloud. A man in a kilt is making a screeching sound with his bagpipes. Ma's idea. The sound drowns out everything. Joey is feeling numb, and it's not from the cold.

People came up to him outside the church to shake his hand and say 'Sorry for your trouble,' but he knows he's the one who should be sorry for the trouble he's caused. Ma said she's proud of him, proud of how he never gave up on Vinnie and proud that he tried so hard to save him. But he didn't save him!

The priest is saying a decade of the rosary and Joey lets his gaze move away from the lip of the grave and sees Detective Brady at the edge of the mourners, mouthing the words of the Hail Mary. There's a space in the crowd beside her and he can see the gravelled pathway down through the grassy plots towards the road. He can see a man in leathers standing down at the gate staring up towards the sombre gathering.

He could be one of the lads from the bike shop or some other dodgy acquaintance of his stepda. The man waves at him. Joey waves back – it's a little secret wave – the back of his hand raised close to his chest.

Then he sees the man hasn't waved. He's just pulling strands of hair away from his eyes. Joey smiles, then feels guilty for smiling. His fingers fold in and he lets his hand fall to his side. He catches Sharon's eye, and she must have seen where he's been looking. They both gaze off towards the road.

There's nobody there now. There's just the growl of a motorbike fading into the distance.

Acknowledgements

This second book has been a long time coming and wouldn't have seen the light of day except for the input from Siobhán Parkinson who saw potential in an early draft and encouraged me to rework it into a far better tale. I am so grateful for her wonderful editing skills that got me out of the way in the telling of the story. I am grateful also to Matthew Parkinson-Bennett and thank you, Kate McNamara, for the welcoming way you have of keeping that bridge open to Little Island. Thanks also to Jack Smyth for the wonderful cover design.

Thanks to Maebh Butler for being first reader who kicked the tyres and gave me the first nod of approval. Thanks to Siobhán Hegarty for having a look under the bonnet and pointing out the bits of rust and the odd rattles that I needed to sort out. Thank you, Tierney Acott who read an early version of the story and helped me steer it in a new direction. Thank you, Fiona O'Rourke for how you lead by example and inspire us all to keep writing. I appreciate you finding two perceptive readers in Tracy and Kitty Kelly who both offered thought provoking feedback when I found myself at a roundabout rather than a crossroads with the story.

Thank you Éile Butler and Mark McGourty for your helpful research.

For my family and friends who thankfully don't ask me too many questions about what I'm writing about because I'm never sure.

Thank you to my Barnstorming Writing Group who continue to offer wonderful writing support, cups of tea and friendship – John A Connolly, Kymberly Dunne-Fleming, Lucinda Jacob and Trisha McKinney.

For my old friends in F-Troupe and for Kathryn Coffey for providing wonderful writing opportunities in the past that kept me writing. And a special thank you to everyone associated with St Anne's National School in Fettercairn, Tallaght, for all the wonderful memories I have of my time there.

But most of all, thank you Gráinne for your constant support for my writing, your patience, and your persistence in encouraging me to be the best writer I can be.

About the Author

James Butler's background is in education and drama. He holds an MPhil in Creative Writing from Trinity College Dublin. He taught in a primary school for many years in Tallaght, Dublin, and set up a Community Drama Theatre Group (F-Troupe) while working there. He wrote plays in collaboration with the group which were performed in the Civic Theatre. In 2005 his play for children *Stuck in the Mud* was nominated for an Irish Times Theatre Award. He spent many years as a writer working in collaboration with the teenage members of Kathryn Coffey's Stage 51 Theatre Group. Some of the plays performed by the group are available on Playshare (Youth Theatre Ireland's curated compendium of plays).

In 2016 his radio play *The Carpet Clown* was produced by *RTÉ Drama On One* as part of The PJ O' Connor Awards.

In 2019 his novel for young adults, *Dangerous Games* was published by Little Island and won the Great Reads Award (2020).

James lives in Dublin with his wife Gráinne.